DEATH

Two Novellas On North American Indians

DANCES

Apple-wood Press

Cambridge 1979

Death Dances © 1979 Apple-wood Press
Wink of Eternity © 1979 John Marvin
The Axing of Leo White Hat © 1979 Raymond Abbott

ISBN: 0-918222-07-9 hardcover
ISBN: 0-918222-08-7 paperback

WINK
OF ETERNITY
By John Marvin

DEATH
wo Novellas On North American Indians
DANCES

THE AXING OF
LEO WHITE HAT
By Raymond Abbott

Contents

WINK
OF ETERNITY
By John Marvin

I

Dr. Ramón Diaz arrived in San Dimas during a festival and then lingered a day in the hotel to prepare for his ordeal: the assignment by the Health Ministry to visit the Tarahumarae Indians, the most remote and non-Westernized tribe in modern Mexico, and if possible, win their trust. They, a remnant of a once prolific race, occupying all of Western Chihuahua, would not welcome this mission for which he had volunteered.

Three days ago he had started through the mountains, the Sierra Madres, eastward by train. Then he had driven about twenty miles over roadless country when, confused by the map, he drove into a wash-out, and the car, an American Jeep, stalled.

He stood now beside the Jeep in the rutted road, a tall man of thirty-five, lean and muscular, darkly Latinate, but with the humane olive eyes of his Yankee mother. Around him the dry plateau lay among midday clarities; to his right were the foothills spotted with bramble and piñon, and immediately on his left the mountains, peak on peak, a pine-sheeted fastness under a roofing of white bedazzling sky.

Bracing himself, he rocked the vehicle in an attempt to dislodge the wheels, until he saw that it was useless. With the impatience of his profession, he swore: "Bastardillo! Chiñgao! God dammit!" Being bilingual served him well in letting off steam. But, he thought, at least he knew the direction to the village.

His white summer suit was streaked with dried mud as he took from the Jeep the suitcase containing his effects and the heavy medical-bag, and thus burdened, began the trek along the winding road of the high mesa. A breeze stirred up a cloud of white alkaloid dust, and his lips were already chapped dry. Yet he felt a sharpening anticipation. He was no sentimentalist, though he would seek to bring what relief he might to an ill-fated and backward race with an infant deathrate of four in five. But that was not his prime motive for being here on this delicate and possibly dangerous errand. Death was the challenge as it had always been for him: his reason for becoming a doctor. In this instance, tribal death. Yet he had a second interest — to explore the past from which he sprang (his father was part-Papago) — he in whom many bloods mingled: Spanish-Moorish, Anglo-Germanic, and farther back, Aztec-Mongol, all the dusts of creation. Also, he felt a vague — what was it? — dissatisfaction or staleness, from working in the tidy, modern hospitals, the routine of a chief-diagnostician, followed by a steak and vintage wine, and a girl a day. The reasons for his choice were clear to him, yet faintly obscure, as if behind them lay some personal emotion or need not quite recognizable.

As he carried the cases, he murmured to himself, " Perhaps, finally, I don't know why. Not absolutamente. But it's no world for absolutes. When *is* one truly alive ... or for that matter, truly dead? In life or in the operating-room, such states are elusive."

He reached a ledge opening into a broad arroyo walled by lovely red and yellow rimrock. He rested, eyes searching, but the gorge was bare of anything except cedars, stone outcroppings, and cacti of many shapes — Turk's-cap, tall saguaro, and agave — as far as his sight could penetrate the low-hung mist. Momentarily, he recalled tales of savagery at the hands of Indians, at which he shrugged. He was too practical-minded, inventive, intent on the present to entertain fears, even of these consummate hunters who could run for days without pause. He believed now that, having studied their language and mores, he would be successful here, just as at Harvard Medical School and during his five-year residency at Mexico City. Beyond that, he knew what he wanted from life—civilized living, cultured women, good music: Bach and Mozart, Chavez and Villa-Lobos. From the time of his mother's early death, he had known his vocation. He knew that medicine could not save mankind; but medicine could allay the suffering and sometimes placate his own death-dread.

As he viewed the plains below, the empty desert shine reflected him to himself—his professional skepticism, his illusionless belief in man, reason, and science, his unbelief in any known God.

Lifting his cases he stalked on. Dust lay on his wrists in soft gray swirls, and he thought: the ladies in Mexico City would twitter to him now, "Ah, Ramón, how pale you have become!" Well, he had always been something of a demon where women were concerned. A dry joke, cheerless out here. As a boy he had been quite a jokester, but medicine sobered one, as did losing one's mother at age ten. But he retained a certain elán—his quick vivacious smile charmed people.

The trail wound downward along the arroyo, and when he glanced back he could no longer see his car stuck in the wash-out. Nothing in sight in the whole landscape, crossed by fluttering heatwaves, but a large tarantula gliding among rock-chips on the ledge. It wriggled off so quickly in the lines of heat that he could not locate its precise point of disappearance. He felt himself suddenly alone, exposed, as if a veil of civilization had been whipped away.

For a while he seemed to walk timelessly along an infinite footpath. Then, somewhere behind him he heard the sound of wheels.

Turning incredulously, he saw the horse and cart bumping up the dusty trail toward him. Outlandish wooden wheels wobbled under the humped form of an Indian on a makeshift seat— undoubtedly one of the Tarahumarae. Quicker than expected the moment of confrontation had come. Sighing, he lowered the luggage and waited, not too tensely. Having chosen to come here alone, all depended on himself. With diplomacy, with ordinary luck, he would persuade the Indian to give him a ride to the village, and afterwards send for the car.

He stood just at the side of the single path and watched as horse, cart, and man approached. High on the seat the huge Indian sat, his face gold-imbued in the bright day, his spectacles (doubtless found somewhere) flashing in the sun. On the flat mesa the cart hung nearly motionless—the sway of the horse's head and fetlock the only sign of progress. As the horse came close, Diaz saw in every detail the driver's hulking form, immense torso, globule thighs, silver-rimmed glasses, one of the lenses cracked.

"Good-day," he said in Spanish, reserving the lingua for a proper time, "I have come as a visitor. May I ride with you to your town?" His smile was decorous and assured as always.

The horse and cart seemed to loom and reach him abruptly, and in amazement he saw that it would not stop. The horse shied where his own head had been as he jerked backward and instantly caught at the reins near the bridle. Slowed by his weight, the cart halted, and he was staring up in wonder and suppressed rage at the man on the seat, the huge round-shouldered Indian who merely sat there and looked down at him emotionlessly, with judicious calm.

"Man, do you not see me here?" Diaz asked the Indian. *"Epa!* Listen! My automóvil does not run, and I have come to visit you. I am a doctor."

The eyes behind the cracked spectacles expressed a merriment and cruelty.

"I can see you," the Indian said. "Now, I ask you who mis-speak our tongue to depart, if you will. Bastante!"

Diaz did not let go the bridle: his fingers loosened, but a refusal to be outfaced, a kind of outrage burning in his veins prevented his letting go. He had come a long way to this, from the Yankee world and the salons of Mexico City, with the same relentless-ness that drove him now. His hands clenched the reins, and he saw the Indian reach and draw out something—a braided snake-whip. The arm swung out, the tapered whip looped through the air, and the thongs forked at him.

He could not have evaded the whip by any means, and he stood without flinching as it struck his shoulder and upper arm a slashing percussive blow. He felt the bite of the thongs leave an imprint along his flesh.

Even then, it was hard for him to believe in the pain, the grieving of his flesh—the fact of it was so bitter, so illogical. In his unyieldingness, all he could do was hold fast to the bridle. He saw the Indian lean to strike again—the immense merry face observing him. Then... nothing. No blow fell as the arm was withheld, and the man looked at him with august scrutiny. At last the Indian spoke.

"Man, I think that you may visit us. That is my judgment."

He could feel his skin cringe and welt where the whiplash had struck, and he could not keep the water out of his eyes, from the pain, the disgust and horror of it. Something (probably his being a doctor) had changed the man's attitude and altered the day. It was borne on him that the stroke of the whip was like an admittance to this world, a queer rite of passage. He moved around the cart and placed the luggage inside it.

"I give you my thanks," he said, his manner again cordial but steely. Bearing the fiery pain, he mounted to the seat beside the Indian and watched as the man flicked the horse's flank with the whip. The small buckskin nag began its jolting walk.

The Indian turned in the seat and appraised him again through the cracked glasses with slow sagacious care and—whatever the amusement signified. Diaz knew that the long look was not meant to be rude, just frankly curious in the manner of Indians. And as Diaz met the stare, he saw in the man's face something quizzical and hurt. Did it reflect personal loss or grief over the slow wreckage of his tribe? Both, probably. A hurtness in the man, so long-felt as to be no longer recognizable to him as despair. Suddenly, the Indian's half-smile reminded Diaz of a death-mask.

Diaz winced as he felt the Indian's grief pass into himself. No comforting vision that! Yet that was precisely why he had come here: to preserve what was left of this tribe if he could. He must not permit horror or mere sympathy to defeat him—that old bugbear. Other medical missionaries and agents who had preceded him had seen some such vision, lost their nerve, and fled. The long scrutiny ended.

"I am Julio." The Indian spoke in deep chest-tones. " I am the *seri-ga-me*, the leader."

Diaz nodded civilly. "I am honored, Julio." He was careful not to offer his hand, knowing the aloofness of these people; except on festive days they kept apart, even from each other, in little spheres of isolation, and they trusted no outlander, Mexican or American. Their withdrawal had preserved them thus far, as race, as an identity. Also he knew why Julio conceived no regret for striking him: to Julio, he was one of the pig-people, the unclean, whose incursions were devouring them.

"I am Dr. Ramón Diaz," he said. "I can heal many diseases, but not all. I would like to stay with your people as a friend." He made no strong pitch, sensing behind the man's pitiless gaze a mind not to be deceived.

"You will meet Maguel," Julio said. "He of the prophecies. And he will listen to you. He alone sees the unseen... the One of evil."

That would be the shaman, Diaz thought. The anointed man who supposedly could view the invisible devil. The man that he must persuade somehow or out-manuever, or out-charm, and eventually overcome.

The cart swayed on, and Diaz, still in pain, decided to respect Julio's cue of silence. It occurred to Diaz that his mission might prove less difficult than he had supposed. The signs were good. Ordinarily, one met resistance from the Indians on two fronts: first, their stoic acceptance of a life-scheme by which their high rate of mortality held the population-growth in check in terms of their means of subsistance; and second, their veneration of the shaman as spiritual leader as well as healer. But judging from his reception this far, their hold on these beliefs must have slackened somewhat. Moreover, the jefe beside him must be a man of much intelligence and a greater than usual concern for human-life.

Diaz drew a handkerchief and wiped his sweat, tidying himself as much as he might. He felt confident now. After all, he had never failed at any important job.

At that moment the trail which the cart straddled dipped downward into the barranca itself. And as he straightened himself on the swaying cart, he saw not more than a quarter-mile below the Indian pueblo. Full in view, the village stood on a sandy basin at the foot of the gorge, a group of low hovels of graystone or weathered wood, hardly distinguishable from the terrain of white sand, yet real, ineluctibly human. It consisted of two concentric rings of dwellings which surrounded a clearing or patio with entrances and exits, and with poles set to mark the patio directions: six of them, north, south, east, west, above, below. The shock of seeing it in all its remote drabness left him in an instant. Judging by the man beside him, what he saw was the husk, not the kernel it contained.

He scented it before he saw it—the cedar smoke rising in faint columns over the village. And he knew that the burning of cedars in summer spelt illness. A terror existed down there, sufficient to cause Julio to bring him here! Instantly, it claimed his whole attention, the probability of cholera or typhoid, the fact of death. He plucked the front of his white jacket away from the sting and throb of the flesh beneath it. Whatever the disease, he could cope with it, if they granted him permission. Fortunately, he carried water purificator and small tins of food in his valise.

Minutes later, after an intensity of waiting, the cart rolled into the street that led to the patio and stopped. He had arrived, near the heart of the pueblo. Beside some of the huts, men sat on stools, each in his spot of solitude, in a kind of self-communion. One by one, their heads turned, and they began to watch Julio and himself. In front of one of the stone-houses (there were five by his count, the remainder were wooden) two women were conversing. Their skirts, wide and white, blew in the breeze. The men wore loincloths or the colorless pajama-like pants, calzones, tied to the ankles, such as Julio was attired in, and white headbands.

As he stepped from the cart the breeze whirred around him, and he could already smell through the cedar smoke, the taint in the air, the fetor as from a latrine, another testimony to the disease. With ponderous slowness, Julio alighted from the cart and spoke to him.

"You will follow me to an empty lodge, *Reko*, if you please."

Diaz took the luggage from the cart and walked behind the Indian who towered a head above any other male in view. They approached one of the huts, built of round gray stones puttied with adobe, a type of *kari-qui* a little finer than the usual wooden ones. Diaz considered: had the previous tenants died of the illness? If so, to them it was a fitting place for him, an outlander engendered of the devil, to await their decision.

Julio stopped at the doorway and gestured to him to go inside. He carried the cases into the shadowed interior and set them down. Behind him, he heard Julio's footsteps moving away, leaving him to himself until the Indian delegation came. Sunblinded, he blinked his eyes to clear them. What he saw was the low-roofed single room, smelling of tribal medicinals, of cedar, and perhaps, ever so faintly, of death. To his left were the fireplace of stone and adobe, reaching to a hole in the roof, and two shelves with bottles and crockery; in the middle of the room a pine table was supported by forked sticks; on the back wall three crosses hung above the bed of goatskins on the slab floor; and in the far corner a round hole served for toilet. The floor of stone was twig-interlaced.

Stooping, he removed the canteen from the case and drank. Then he sat down on a sapling-woven stool facing the entrance. A moment later, there came a knock at the partly closed door.

The man who entered and stepped up to him was of average height, stocky but not plump. A black sombrero with fine needlework at the brim, a touch of lace, hung by a string across his shoulders, and his long black hair clustered on his neck like a woman's. Diaz immediately noticed the man's eyes—they were calm and sweet, yet manly and direct.

"I am Luis Oma, the hunter," he said in soft Indian. "I am told that you are the médico, and I have one who is not well...if you will please come."

This was the test, Diaz surmised.

"Good," he said, taking up the medical bag. "Lead me there."

He followed Luis Oma outside into the curiously glaring sunlight, the effect of the white sands and the lack of any shade. He became intently observant. The malodor rose on the light wind, and he could tell that it came from nearby and from the south. Luis Oma led him across the peyote patio to one of the primitive wood-shelters, hardly more than ten feet long, rectangular with two forked uprights to hold the top-beam. There were windows, but no doors. Oma merely removed two rough boards, and they went inside.

In the dank gloom of the hovel an old woman lay on a skin pallet. Across the room, a young woman was seated before a slow-burning cedar fire, her back to him. He placed the heavy case on the table and removed the flashlight. When he shone the light on the old woman's face he saw that she was dying.

A movement behind him diverted his attention. The young woman in her swishing skirt floated out of the shadows and knelt noiselessly by the old woman. In the cone of light, Diaz saw that despite her gracefulness she was not beautiful, though in her full-cheeked soft face and her languorous eyes there was some uncommon charm.

"This one who lies there," Luis Oma said, "is my grandmother. This little one...(the gaiety of his smile flashed out)... is Rosalina, Rosa-lee-na, my cousin...a much in a little."

Diaz greeted her with a slight bow. "Will you help me, Rosalina?" Without waiting for an answer he added peremptorily, "Uncover her chest and arms, please."

Rosalina's quick and supple hands exposed the old woman. Absorbed, Diaz worked swiftly over her in her comatose state. The pulse was low, the skin oozed an edema. When he bent low, he

detected the evil mephitic scent. She might be a few hours from
death's balm. If healing her were the test, he must inevitably fail.
The malady was typhoid.

"You are right, she is not well," he said. "I have come too late.
She has a disease, typhoid, and death is near. Keep her warm
until then."

Luis Oma's candid sweet-eyed stare did not leave his face for a
long moment.

"Your words echo truth," Luis Oma stated at last. "We will keep
her warm."

The girl spoke unexpectedly. "With my tears," she said in a
tone of mourning. "And my own breath."

Startled by her depth of feeling, by the young man's apparent
foreknowledge of the woman's condition, he replaced the
instruments in the bag. In an obscure way he guessed that he had
passed, at least, a first obstacle here, a trial of honesty. Leaning,
he covered the old woman snugly in her stage of chill, and
adjusted her head. Her toothless mouth and fluttering eyes were
restful in expression, fast asleep. When he straightened, Luis
Oma had vanished, and the girl sat on the stool in front of the
fireplace, her back to him as before.

Diaz went through the aperture into the omniscient sunlight in
which all externals and pretenses tended to fade and realities
alone remained. Walking slowly across the baked sand of the
patio, he thought: if the epidemic were too far advanced, most of
the people might die. Had he come here a few days too late, to
oversee the death of the village? No one was in sight as he
reached the *kari-qui* and entered it. Once inside, he slumped in
sudden melancholy to the stool. Something — a quality in the
people, a quietude beyond despair, as old as mankind itself —
had unleashed his emotions. Abruptly, he heard footsteps and
men appeared at the door. They began to file into the lodge:
Julio, immense and round-shouldered, followed by Luis Oma
and by a slender, gray-eyed newcomer. The last to enter was a
small bearded man of about forty, obviously a half-breed or
mestizo, who wore huarches and carried a long-necked bottle.

They stood against the wall in silent assemblage, all but the little half-caste who crouched with the bottle beside him.

Diaz stood up, and Julio spoke to him.

"We men of the Daramuli, as we name ourselves, are ready to talk to you now." He pointed to the man next to him, the slender Indian with a fine sinewy face, eyes like gray smoke. "Here is Juano Amezcuo who has been to school and writes of our past."

Juano Amezcuo, stepping forward, suddenly extended his hand and barely touched Diaz's fingers.

"*Dios Kuira*, Doctor," he said with grave courtesy. " God goes with you."

Julio's look became again cruelly judicious with its mask of glee. "And this man is Maguel," he said, gesturing toward the little half-caste. "He who deals in talismans and dreams, and heals those whom evil betides."

Diaz saw Maguel clearly now—the slight figure squatted there, the dreamy but alert eyes, the short beard neatly contoured around a birthmark, which lent a peculiar pathos to his smile.

"Good day, Señor Médico," Maguel said in his too-quiet voice. "Como está usted?" There was mockingness in his use of the Spanish.

It was Juano Amezcuo who commented, "Maguel is our single *yowami*, healer. The other one, who is with death, lived here in this *kari-qui*."

Poised, easeful, Diaz greeted him with a nod. This then was the shaman—either a fraud or a man of acumen who enacted the role of healer and performed the rituals. Looking at Maguel he had the impression of intelligence and natural superiority thwarted by chance and primitiveness. It was a harsh moment; he, Dr. Ramon Diaz, was here to strip the yowami's ancient prerogative, and Maguel must know that. But they had granted him some kind of privilege. Diaz's manner was urbane, but uncompromising.

"We are alike only in that we make men well," he said to the little man. "I have no gift of prophecy."

Maguel was studying him with his fixed melancholy smile. He wore a clean blouse, but his calzones were filthy, stained with sweat, dust, perhaps urine and blood. Maguel, still squatting, lifted the bottle and with long, adept fingers removed the stopper and drank. Then he brushed the mouth of the bottle with his palm, with an almost finical care.

"Luis Oma has belief in you," Maguel said. He held out the bottle without moving from his place, as if deliberately forcing Diaz to come to him. Diaz, showing no vexation, stepped forward, took the bottle, and drank sparingly. It was tesgüino, something like Mexico City beer. He returned the bottle, and as he straightened he saw them all regarding him with utterly frank curiosity. Then he heard Maguel speaking.

"Four of us died this fortnight, and eight have the sickness." His smile flitted over the men against the wall, as if half in sympathy, half in mockery of their grief. "The dead, they are dead ...*suwiami*. We will care for the living." His eyes touched Diaz' face with subtle malice. "You decide, Julio, that this man will help us end the outlanders' disease. I agree to this."

Glancing at the others...Julio, Oma, and Amezcuo—he could sense the greatness of their need which had led them to forego for a time their beliefs and traditions. For himself, it was an entrance into their world where medicine and faith were indivisible, so that to convert them to his science he must subvert their religion. He could not suppress a pity, almost a wish that it need not be.

"You have honored me," he said. "Thank you for your trust." His smile was cordially sincere.

They were silent. Always taciturn, they neither overspent nor misused words. Juano Amezcuo found his tongue first.

"*Beari bache ba*," he said. "Until tomorrow."

He and Luis Oma went outside, disappearing into the stillness, and Julio and Maguel stepped one by one into the direct sunlight where they stopped. Diaz, following, stood in the doorway. Facing him, they remained speechless, self-immersed in their differing ways. Then Julio, in the manner of his people, began to turn sidewise, by degrees, away from Diaz until his whole broad back was turned to him. No insult was implied; it was only an habitual vigilance against enemies, stalkers.

"The cornfield burns," Julio stated to Maguel. "The evil wind is on the land and on us."

Diaz, conscious of the tainted breeze, looked out over the small plots of stunted corn on the bottomland to the west. The stalks were withered, the long leaves turning russet, and even he knew that they were earless, barren. He noticed under a nearby shed a few brown stalks of last year's corn, its leaves rattling. Beyond the fields on the rocky hillsides a few goats, brown and white, cropped the stubble-grass.

"It is the *chabo-chi*," Maguel said, spitting the words. "The devil seeks to dry up our seed."

Julio and Maguel were facing Diaz, but they avoided looking at him. They knew that he understood: the *chabo-chi* was the devil, but the name was synonymous with Mexican or white man.

"The rain will fall," Maguel said, his dreamily wry smile passing over them. "I will see to that. The deadness will pass." He began to walk away, without a parting word. Mountebank or man of subtlety or both, he walked rapidly but without apparent haste. There was just the whisper of his huarches on the hard earth of the patio.

Julio's face was impassive with the apparently timeless sorrow.

"Maguel is a good *yowami*," Julio said, "but he cannot end the foreigner's disease. Your people ascend to the skies while we shrink to living stones." A look of fatalistic repose came over him. "I have seen what you médicoes can do. A man with a horse will pull your automóvil here, and tomorrow you will go with me to the *kari-qui* of the people."

Diaz had rehearsed to himself what he must say. "I can cure the disease," he told Julio, "if you will let me use needles, and if I can find the place from whence the contagion comes."

"No fear have I of you, though others fear," Julio said. " At my word, the people will do as you ask...but they will not understand." Julio's back was toward him now. "Food and drink will reach you soon." He plodded off toward another stone-house which must be his own.

For a time Diaz did not move from the doorway. Long shadows from the poles crisscrossed the patio, the sacred ground, and by the time his car arrived it would be night. Re-entering the hut, he glanced around with careful objectivity. He would utilize this place as headquarters but find another empty one for a hospital; and he would have to work quickly to save these people and implant his own seed of modernism here. He recognized a danger, present all around him in the rarefied Sierra air; it emanated from the little shaman and from the distrust of the people. In sober fact they had turned against outsiders and hunted them to the earth like pigs: the sun-embalmed or kite-eaten bodies of bandidos and intruders had been found cleanly knifed and hung by thews to trees. And some kind of personal struggle between Maguel and himself must ensue. But he was aware of no actual fear; his own weapon of science was, in its way, keener.

Mindful again of the fretful burn of the whiplash across his shoulder, he took off his jacket and shirt. Naked to the waist he examined the long reddish-purplish welt across his upper body, and bore its undercurrent of pain. It would suppurate a little where the skin was broken. He opened the bag hurriedly and smeared zinc-oxide over the ridge of flesh. He would have suffered a greater scourging to be here, anything less than martyrdom.

Afterwards, he drew on a clean white shirt. He began to place on the warped pine-knotted shelves the few instruments and medicines he would need here.

II

At nine o'clock that night he was standing in the doorway and smoking a cigarillo while the azure evening descended over the barranca. The front of his car was visible where it stood flush to the lodge's side. It had been dragged here, unharmed, and he had taken from it the ice-chest containing perishable drugs. After eating the tinned food, he was able to think with total clarity, to sift his emotions. What he had not counted on was his attraction to these people; they were different from the Indians of his imagination or memory. Allowing for centuries of isolation, they possessed a culture, however opposed to his own. Something in them drew him beyond mere challenge. He would have to discern what it was.

A coyote yelped from a near mountain slope which lay in dense purple. There was no other sound but the hiss of his Coleman lamp. Abruptly, a man came into the square of light and stopped before him — a squat powerful Indian with a round childlike face.

"My name is Rojas," the man said with great shyness. " Maguel wishes you to come with me."

He nodded and stepped back to take up his flashlight. For an instant he thought of trickery, but he must take the risk, show absolute trust. He went outside, and Rojas, without further words, began to lead him across a corner of the patio toward a near stone-house. The moon was up; its pallid disc overtopped the blackened mountains, like an omphalos.

"I am taking you to see Maguel's lodge," Rojas said. " Soon we will go where he is."

There was no hint of a trap, and he followed Rojas into the shelter. A cedar log blazed in the fireplace, and an oil-lamp burned on the table. A woman with very long black hair, undoubtedly Maguel's wife, sat by the fireplace and did not look around at them.

Rojas, in embarrassment, stepped aside. Diaz realized that he was being accorded a kind of courtesy, though behind it was Maguel's cunning mind. He walked past the dining table to another shorter stand. On it, laid out in order, were surgical tools of bone and stone, bronze and iron, several of them centuries old: knives of various shapes, scissors, trocars, crude saws and needles 3 to 20 cm. in length. This was what the shaman intended him to see. In the second row were blunt instruments, hammers, tubes, forceps, catheters. He forebore touching them. Works of marvelous handicraft, some of them were suitable for present use. A feeling of near-reverence came to him from seeing this heirloom of the years. He was vaguely saddened by his own presence there which reduced all this to obsolescence.

Surveying the implements, he could determine the breadth of the little man's practice. He could set bones, drain abscesses, extract bullets or other foreign bodies, stitch wounds. This was not necromancy, but surgery.

The skull itself rested on the rear of the table. Immediately, he saw that it was not a mere death's head. In the brain pan were two precisely spaced holes, trepanned there by an expert and sensitive hand. And beside the skull was the trephin, the bone-auger used to drill the holes.

Rojas drew closer in his shy, not timid, way.

"The openings are for those with fevered minds or swellings of great pain," Rojas said. "The Yowami has worked on many such. Most lived until old age, but this one died in the cutting. Maguel looks at it often."

Diaz could guess what disturbed the shaman: death had occurred without apparent cause, one of the medical mysteries. It was clear to him that the man was no mere quack; such an operation would take hours, possibly days, that much patience and finesse. He scanned the decanters of medicines: powdered herbs, vervain, hemlock, and the bottled peyote and mescal which they believed sacred.

"We can go now," he said to Rojas. As they went out, the woman sat unmoving before the fire.

Rojas, who had seized the flashlight like a toy, switched it on and darted the beam to and fro in the twilight, in joyous pagan arcs. They came to a wood shelter, its entrance open, and they stepped inside.

Maguel, in the soiled trousers, sat on a stool beside the pallet of a sick middle-aged man. Diaz pressed near enough to see that the man's naked upper body was mottled with fever, his eyes glazed, lifeless, his body in extreme debility, and respiration had almost ceased. Ashes had been applied to the man's forehead and chest, so that they formed a light coating. Nothing could save the man now, not the finest antibiotics and intravenous feeding.

From his cloth bag, Maguel took a bottle of the mescal and anointed the man's face and throat with soft touches. After that, with the help of a heavy, strong-armed woman, the shaman began wrapping the man in a sweat-skin. It was, Diaz thought, a futile act which might mercifully induce a quicker death. He was seeing here the first instance of these people's need, of the *yowami's* abuses. The man should not be dying! Anger, disgust soared in him, and the narrow back of the mestizo filled his sight. Bending over the nearly dead man, Maguel spoke.

"Listen to me, Tio!" His voice was sharp, yet tender. " You will live, my friend." Then, more insistent. "Do you hear my words, Tio? You will live! Do you believe me?"

Into the emaciated face there came some bare glimmer of partial awareness. Nothing after that.

Diaz touched Rojas' shoulder. "I must return to my lodge," he said. "If you please."

Rojas inclined his head, and unattended, Diaz left the hovel. Moving through the evening hush, he reasoned that Tio's case must be crucial to Maguel, else the *yowami* would not have summoned him there. His disgust passed; he knew now the extent of Maguel's skills and of his failures. But he found that he could not reason about Maguel — he felt, at the same instant, drawn and repulsed by the man, as by two opposing lodestones.

His own hut threw its white radiance toward him. Tomorrow could be endless; tonight, he must try to sleep.

But lying on the hard pallet under a jet of moonlight, sleep evaded him. He felt that the smart of the whip's laceration was merely the outward cause of his restlessness. An emergency existed: someone might be catching the fever that instant or someone else dying while he lay here, in effect, debarred from practice. Damnation! It all smacked of fatalism and waste — neither of which he could stomach.

For another thing, here in this alien place, his mind kept fleeing back to old haunts in sudden visions that jerked him awake.

Sparrows were pecking crumbs from the brownstone window in Oaxaco, and the boy watching them was himself, while downstairs his mother sang "Casta Diva" from *Norma*. Here, in this obscure hut he heard her beautiful voice as his other self fed the sparrows.

That scene blinked out. Then he reached under his anatomy book and tossed seeds to a robin outside on one of Harvard's snowbanks — another self, another bird, his mother's voice long since silenced. From leukemia, possibly curable some day. The young man with the medical books missed his homeland hardly at all. By then, if not actively anti-Latin-American, his sympathies were increasingly Yankee. How could one admire Spanish-American dictators, palace revolutions, sloth, poverty, indifference to life itself? "*Mañana*," the Mexican said to him, settling himself under his sombrero, meaning "*Never*."

Wide awake, he turned on his left side away from the moonlight. A voice cried, *"Niño!"* That was his real Spanish duenna in Philadelphia where his father was Mexican consul. The American kids with whom he was playing garbled the word. *"Hey, ninny!"* Then he was running inside with his first bloody nose. The duenna said, *"Sangre de Cristo!"* So long ago when he was twelve — yesterday.

Lying on his back again, he recalled a summer vacation in Spain. *"Here is our true heritage,"* his father said proudly. Walking up Madrid's streets, he saw Generalisso Franco's soldiers at parade-rest. Leaning on a rotten fence, he viewed the Escurial, dreaming of Emperor Philip and of the lost empire, the Spanish Armada, and the rest. Pieces of a heritage at best. Grand schemes, whether Philip's or Montezuma's, seemed to end in dead monuments to be visited by touristas. Christ Himself was such a monument. What was one to make of inquisitions, communism, fascism, Napoleon, Stalin, Hitler, Franco, Zapata, and so on? Nothing. Nada. Any hope lay in the present. The past was a grave, and the future was "mañana."

A line of a childhood prayer came to him: "Everything passes." The absurd prayer, repeating in his mind, began to bring on sleep...

III

The morning dawned in pale and dewy tones of gold and lavender. He lingered by the open door, having eaten the canned food and dressed in fresh white trousers and shirt. A gulf of silence encompassed all the morning sounds — a single cockcrow, the whimper of a child somewhere, and the sporadic barking of a dog. It was time to make his first foray.

Going outside, he walked past the gray shapes of corn-bins and the outer circle of hovels. Ahead of him the path was littered with the pulp of cardboard boxes and rusted cans, evidence of a foregone flirtation with the Mexican world. Pausing, he watched the sunrise between the two highest peaks. There glowed a corona of light, though on the slopes the madroños and cedars were cast in violet. He was viewing now the emergence of the tribe's god-sun, just as last night he had strolled under their goddess-moon. Did such fantasies enrich the believer? For him, the esthetic modern, they sweetened the mind like a kind of cathartic. In the midst of it all lay the main question.

"Ramón Diaz," he murmured. "Why are you the *one* to be here?"

No complete answer. Before him in the new light were the barren fields and beyond them the mountain escarpments, peopleless and sempiternal. He was alone in a naked land, and there was no refuge. How, he wondered, had this proud people adapted itself to the exposure, the poverty, the unhope?

He began to walk downhill toward a spruce-fringed creek, its narrow band of water beginning to glisten in the first sunlight. Later, he would have to sample all the sources of water. In another minute, he stood on a hillock above the stream, an unstinted flow of crystalline water. But he saw on a mesa, just below, a pond into which it emptied, and further downhill a second smaller pool. In one of these the disease lurked.

He had taken a step to leave when he noticed the burial ground. It spread out on the slope above the second, smaller pool, and consisted of a score of mounds heaped with stone. Immediately, he guessed the truth. Some of the graves were very close to the pool's edge, and he surmised that drainage underground — rivulets of rainwater washing over and through the corpses — was the contaminant. Horribly and quite simply the fact leered at him. Once, in a halcyon time, the Indians had developed immunities to such diseases, but contact with the Spanish invaders had lent to all germs a new virulence. His face hardset, he moved up the path.

He had just gone inside his lodge when he heard someone approach, and Julio, by himself, stood at the open door. His eyes behind the cracked spectacles were abrupt, jagging.

"Good-day, Médico," he said. "Will you go to the not-well?"

His own smile became bladed.

"If you, seri-ga-me, will tell the people not to drink from the small lake. I think that the water is foul."

The huge man studied him without apparent belief or disbelief. "A messenger will be sent soon," he said, "to all the men and women."

Diaz took up the lighter medical bag and went with him. In the intense brightness of the morning, the breeze picked at the white dust, and the latrinal odor arose, saturating the once soft air. With lime, he would quell the scent. Yet anxiety worked at his mind in new ways. One error or mischance traced to him might lead to his failure with the people. It was to the nearest shack across the street that Julio directed him. A man and woman of middle-age were standing by the door, and Julio addressed them.

"This outlander is a *yowami*. He will heal your son."

The man and woman shrank from Diaz, and the man, stolid and glaring, shook his head. The woman, her eyes very brilliant and hot, thrust her hands at him.

"*Chati!*" she cried. "The evil!"

"No," Julio said to her. "You will permit him to go inside." He touched the man's shoulder. "And you, Luna, I would have you bear a message."

Unwillingly, grudgingly, the woman gave way, and Julio took the man aside. Diaz could see along the row of shacks other Indians observing this extraordinary and fearful happening. Nerveless, undeviating, he went inside.

The interior was clean, neat, like most of the huts a marvel of economy, the art of living in poverty. A boy of twelve lay on goatskins, his mouth open, moaning in delirium. Seating himself on a stool, Diaz began the examination. Skin dry and fiery, pulse rapid, the syndrome of typhoid.

"Has he the evil you speak of?" Julio's voice demanded.

"Yes," he answered, using an ophthalmoscope. "The same one." Glancing up, he saw the broad face break with grief. For that moment, the hauteur and perspicacity crumbled into sadness.

He introduced a rectal thermometer, but without waiting for a reading, he prepared a sedative. The woman and Julio hovered closer. Unable to hold the boy's shifting head, he hurriedly administered the hypo. At the sight of the needle, the mother groaned, and he saw on Julio's brow sparkles of sweat.

A short time later the boy's threshings and convulsions eased and then ended. Diaz withdrew the thermometer: 105.1 degrees of fever, but the boy would survive.

"Rest now, muchacho mío," he said, out of his habitual sympathy for any sufferer. When he stood up, the woman made room for him with sudden respect, silenced by magic.

"The fever should cool soon," he said crisply. "I can make him well." As he spoke, he realized that he had strayed into a false pride through some latent snobbery and vainglory which he shared with every shaman. Naked to himself in a denuded world, he heard Julio say, "That is good. Twice good."

Annoyed at his self-surveillance, he followed the jefe outside into the excoriating sunlight. The day would be long, with no time for paltry scruples. A bitterness pervaded him as it always did when facing disease, death. But in him was a kind of detachment, the part of him which remained unrelated to anything except the work at hand (he thought of it as the genius of Western man) which tempered any disaster.

At the next house, a strongly built woman confronted them, her arms crossed over her heaving breasts. She blocked the doorway.

"He will not enter!" she panted. "He and his people are the cause of all disease."

Julio held up his palm, saying, "Who is best able to cure his disease than the bearer? Stand aside, woman!"

She permitted Diaz to squeeze into the lodge.

Inside was squalor. Two small naked children played on a urine-soaked mud-floor. He stepped around them to where the man, obviously the father, lay unclothed except for a breechclout, a fleshless breathing skeleton. Diaz himself was shaken. This hut was not typical: the family clearly prostrated by the ordeal of lingering death.

A moment later, after a cursory check, he saw that the man was not to be helped. T.B., the terminal phase, and ironical, because the man might well have contracted it from outlanders. All that could be done was move him, when possible, to a place of isolation.

"This man has a disease of the lungs," he told Julio. "He can bring death to others. He must be moved from here soon."

Julio bowed his head, and Diaz, looking down at the slimed floor had a moment's sensation of nausea.

As he started to walk out behind Julio, the brazen-faced woman came toward him, her arms akimbo. Darting her head at him, she spat straight into his face.

Halting, he rebuffed her snakelike frenzy with his own sympathetic elan. But inside, he felt humbled, and he resisted the itching urge to wipe the spittal from his cheek until he had squeezed through the exit, the hole in the wall. As he applied the hankerchief, he thought that maybe it was good to feel once again humility.

Julio, who had seen the obsenity, paused beside him.

"I apologize," he said. "The woman is not bad. She has a great soul, but she is troubled."

Diaz nodded. "I will speak with her at another time."

Julio preceded him up the white street. In the doorways the women stood. Their skirts, white and wide, blew in the breeze. Some wore a *kemaka* or light serape over one shoulder. Passing them, he smiled his best and nodded to each, receiving in answer their dark-eyed aversion. He noticed their ornaments — the plain talisman at the throat to ward off sickness, ear-beads of jade, exposed by their long swept-back black hair. Suddenly, their lack of cosmetics made them appear to Diaz more real, in some sense, than the elegant girls of his acquaintance.

Julio paused before another house of sickness.

It was evening before he finished the rounds. Seated at his own table, he was weary, yet elated — he had impressed Julio and some of the people and accomplished things. He had worked with the special care of a highly skilled diagnostician, and he had found five new cases of typhoid, one of gangrene (he had given the tetanus shot and cleansed the necrotic tissue) a terminal case of T.B., and another of coronary occlusion. He had faced hatred and moved among menacing shadows. Twice he had fronted men with knives in their belts. He lighted a cigarillo and attempted to relax, while the Coleman lamp hissed in the wilderness

With terrific suddenness, Julio appeared in the tide of light and advanced to the table. The man's face wore a paradox of gratitude and regret.

"I believe that you were a good médico where you come from." Julio waved his hand toward the darkness. "You did not need to be told of one man's lungs or another man's heart. You are one of the inspired." He held out his palms. "Tell me what you wish to be done."

Diaz blew smoke through the hard-drawn line of his lips. He had expected this much acceptance, no more. Now, he would have to make the man understand the difficulties.

"I need someone to go to the nearest town farmacia and bring these things." He pointed to the prescription slips on the table. "I need, too, another Mexican doctor and a nurse to assist me."

Julio's look became dubious — then he turned his head from side to side. "That cannot be. Maguel will not agree to permit other outlanders here," he answered.

Diaz thought: the voice of the politician and compromiser, though this one was without duplicity. Yet it stung him like the downlash of the whip. Maguel's influence must not prevail. It was time to play his own hand.

"I could refuse to stay unless I have helpers," he stated. Imperious, relentless, he confronted the Indian. "In that case, many would die. I would hate to be the cause of death."

Julio sighed heavily, and his mouth hardened into cruelty.

"And I would hate, too, having to send hunters to bring you back," Julio said. "But I would have to do that, Medico!"

Diaz kept his composure, but clearly he had lost. Given the chance, the young mescaleros would run him down like a deer. Julio's hand was still the one that held the whip.

"Then I will need the help of Luis Oma and his cousin Rosalina."

Julio held up his hand as a pledge of agreement. After that, he took up the prescriptions, stepped into the black doorway, and paused.

"Rojas will run all night to bring the medicine." He spoke over his shoulder. "Tío, whom Maguel watched over, is well. His fever is gone and he talks. But Tío is only one." Julio stalked out.

Gripped by near-unbelief of the news of Tío, Diaz propped himself a moment against the table. It was like hearing an untruth cloaked as truth or the inverse, since Julio's honesty was absolute. To his memory came the moribund man, ashes on his arms and chest, and Maguel bent over him crying out: "You will live, Tío." But actually the man should have died. He pondered it. Such recoveries sometimes occurred; there was an unpredictability underlying life and death which rendered all prognosis relative. Had Maguel induced in Tío a great life-wish and somatic change? Was there some kind of empathy between the doctor and patient? Diaz lifted his shoulders and let them slump again. Any such resurrection was purely natural. Yet there was no question of Maguel's gift: he was acquainted with that other, call it spiritual, dimension. It changed nothing, the yowami's single success with typhoid, and as for himself, the people would notice that the recoveries (all but this one) and the expiration of the disease coincided with his coming there.

Going to the door, he saw the shimmer of oil-lamps and candles in the windows of the nearer lodges. So, he would lack professional assistance here and be on his own. He was about to close the door when someone came toward him in the semi-dark — it was the tall Indian who had been to school, Juano Amezcuo. Now fully in the light, Amezcuo smiled at him.

"Let us go to the rutuburi, the sacred dance," Juano said. "It lifts both the mind and the body."

He returned a smile feeling an immediate closeness to the young man who, by some means, had become the scribe of an unwritten language.

"I accept your invitation with pleasure," he answered in Mexican. He closed the door behind him, and Juano Amezcuo, thin-faced, eyes smoky gray, motioned in the direction of the patio.

IV

When Diaz and Juano Amezcuo rounded the row of huts, the dance-place was lighted on all sides. Torches were hung from poles at each of the six patio-directions, and boy acolytes were tending them. Diaz saw that the women were assembled to the south-end — girls from early puberty to old women, they were the dancers or chorus — and the men lined the sides as onlookers. The altartable, a flat plank without ornament, was to the east, and a small cross with an avatar of meat was placed by the altar to "feed sickness". Diaz, warmed by the sight, spoke first.

"You Darimuli will live through these evil days."

The glow from the patio gave an incandescence to Amezcuo's lean features.

"The Darimuli may live, and their spirit may die," Amezcuo answered. "The doors to death are without number." A sadness without bitterness caught at his lips. "That is why I write of the people with my left hand. If it happens that no one remains to see my words but those of outlandish blood, I hope that they will not fling my words to the winds. You understand? Tu sabés."

The thought of tribal liquidation hurt Diaz more personally than ever before. Yet Juano Amezcuo, as if flinging off a cloud, became gay, frolicsome among the serious faces. To Diaz, he said, " The *rutuburi* will begin soon. Maguel is coming."

Maguel, dressed in a black blouse, but the same white, stained trousers, stopped on the west side. On his head was a circlet of feathers and in each hand a rattle which he sounded rhythmically. Behind him, Luis Oma bore a jar which must contain peyote or the mescal. Luis Oma wore a dark red serape across one shoulder.

"The dance is for many purposes," Juano Amezcuo said. " To ask the gods for aid, to cause them to descend to earth. Also, to honor the dead, to cure fields and men, and to conjure the rain. The one in the all... the all in the one."

The women had lined up Indian file, facing west toward Maguel fronting them, his face to the east. Each woman's right hand was clasped in the left hand of the woman in front of her.

There came a long silence, and the stars in the black sky were very close and bright like the festooned roof of an enormous tent.

At last Maguel moved. He beat the rattle, the *ariki*, in an up and down movement and began to sing or chant —

Se-wa-ga-wiri, waka waka

Immediately, the women in the line swung their bodies in harmony, and their rattling belts rustled in unison. In the dance-step, the woman's left foot was placed forward, then the right followed by a slight jump and a single foot-beat on the ground as the right foot joined the left, all in accord to the shaman's movements.

For Maguel it was a triple performance: music-maker, singer, and dancer. For a while, only the simple rhythmic step.

Then, from a crouched position, Maguel sprang upward and outward, arms out-thrust while snapping the *ariki* and chanting. With effortless agility, his upper body rigid, he executed a series of leaps. The third leap brought him to the altar. The women, linked as before, performed a slow step or shuffle, a delicate counterpoint to the shaman's actions, like a sarabande.

Diaz watched in sudden pleasure. Maguel made the return leaps, another triad, and then repeated the sequence, with the same effect of controlled violence, measure and counter-measure, strophe and antistrophe. Diaz noticed that by degrees the leaps took on a vestige of agony which seemed to elicit in himself a kind of kinesthesia, a sense of taking part.

"You see that it is very good," Juano Amezcuo said. "Like mescal."

Diaz saw in the man's demeanor his own reaction. Like himself, Juano was drawn to the spectacle, the esthetic exterior, though to the Indian more must be meant.

"For me, it is like tequila," Diaz answered. He tried to make out the mode of the paen or chant: it resembled Dorian, but it was probably older, perhaps Mongol.

At that point, Maguel halted and took the crock, the chalice, from Oma. As he drank from it, one of the men blew an old horn, a klaxon, and its raucous blare broke the severe silence. Maguel looked off into the crowd and responded with his smile of pathos and a shake of the rattles.

Rutuburi we yena!

Chanting, Maguel began the dance as before — but after the third soaring leap, he stopped between the above-pole and the below-pole and motioned to the altar-tenders. They carried two torches to him, and he took them and knelt with the faggots upheld in each hand. With theatric quickness he sprang up and began a bizarre display of twirls and stands, motion and stasis. He danced as if hallucinated, no doubt affected by the mescal. And gradually his arms drew the torches closer to his upper body until the flames licked at his sides, and his features grimaced in torment. Then he began to spin, so that for ten or more seconds he half disappeared into the whirling rondure of fire. Absorbed by it, Diaz saw Maguel begin to slow, and the wheel of flame disintegrated as he hurled the firebrands high into the night skies. They fell, scattering sparks around the slight stationary figure. In the shaman's face there was no suggestion of pain —

though he must be injured—instead a mien of rapture. Diaz wondered: to what extent had the peyote inspired the man?

Thinking of it, Diaz understood the principle of the dance. It was no prayer to the gods; it was an incantation that forced the gods down to earth. The *Yowami*, by a pride and power, controlled the gods and hence his own fate. In his solitary fire-pillar, he had burned without being consumed. To Diaz it was a splendid fantasy. Paranoia with grandiose delusions would be the clinical description of the shaman, if that mattered.

Juano Amezcuo was talking to someone else, and Diaz departed alone. He had witnessed an ordinary ceremony, apart from the fire-dance; but its happening just at this time indicated that Maguel meant to claim any future healings, meant to steal his, the foreigner's, magic. Yet Maguel would not be able to explain why so few recovered before Diaz arrived.

Inside the hut, he took his single precaution of placing the Indian wedge in the door; he had no physical fear except the remote one of a collusion to kill him. What bothered him was the sense of being an intruder into their destiny. He reflected that, left to itself, the disease would run its course, hastening by a little the day when the Tarahumarae would cease to be. But had they a right to choose their own fate? Their retreat to this bare life to avoid the cutthroat outer world, the destruction brought on by racial pollution, had failed. The diseases, including their own paranoia, continued apace, and even their *yowami* was a half-caste. Diaz felt that his mission was clear; yet he remained an interloper.

He poured tesgüino into a paper cup and sipped it. He was certain that these people mattered to him; he had seen all day their virtues —candor, peace, cooperation, courtesy, fortitude. But certain darker intimations about himself in relation to the Indians were submerged, just outside recognition.

He finished the nightcap and began stripping off his clothes.

V

Dawn and noon passed like repetitions of the first ones; apart from small variations, they might have been parts of an infinite day. During his rounds, he found the boy, Ignazio, whose convulsions he had stopped, was now clear in mind and convalescing, though the granulation of his lips was too severe for him to speak. The other patients were alive, even Luis Oma's grandmother lingered. At past noon, Rojas arrived with the vaccines — dust-coated, round-countenanced, indefatigable, Rojas had been running for over twelve hours. By mid-afternoon Diaz had inoculated half the village and had strewn a bag of lime over the odoriferous latrines.

Alone now, he walked through the lucid monochrome of the day. Ahead of him he saw Luis Oma seated by himself on a stool outside his house, his attitude one of quiet reflection, of aloneness without loneliness. As Diaz approached, the man's attention turned to him, and he stood up. Under the brim of the black-laced sombrero, Oma regarded him with his sweet-eyed gaze.

"I have heard of Ignazio," Luis Oma said. "The one who lives because of you. I am ready to offer my hands to you."

Diaz showed his gratitude. "It is appreciated," he said. " Would you like to go to my house for a drink? It will be a long day for us."

The Indian shook his head, but with a look of warm regard. " Thank you, no. I do not mind the length of days."

Diaz studying him felt an envy of Oma's serene temperament and an affection that was like love—another sign of his involvement with these people.

"You remain here sometimes for half a day," he said to Oma.

"I have happiness sitting here," Oma answered. "There is much for one to see...our ancestors, the animals, the birds, the stones. In them too we see ourselves as we will become, and in our children ourselves as we were. While in the skies the gods of day and night are as they have always been. All things are here within the circle of the horizon."

Diaz tried to imagine it: the simplicity and unity which for him could never exist. For him, the diverse and changeful were the stuff of life. He was bothered, too, by the young man's gentleness which never betrayed anger or any quality other than faith, openness, and candor. Was any such saintliness ultimately opposed to his own outlook?

"Here is what we must do," he said to Oma. "Will you bring to my *kari-qui* a bottle of water from every place where water is found and used here? Also, I want an empty *kari-qui* washed with soap...(he pointed to the red can of disinfectant just outside his own lodge)...and four beds made inside it with the blankets which are in my car. Later, Rosalina can help with the unwell."

Luis Oma's tranquil almond eyes showed no doubt of him.

"These things I am able to do," he said. "After that, Rosalina will come to you."

Diaz, with a nod, hurried off through the dazzle of light. He went inside the shelter and seated himself at the table where he began to scribble names, dates, diagnoses. As he ground out his cigarette, he glanced up and saw Maguel in the doorway.

Dressed in the variously soiled trousers, Maguel came inside. Naked above the waist except for an amulet round his neck, Maguel gave no greeting. A smile, melancholy but ruthless, played at his lips above the irregular neatness of the beard.

"I am told that you have a name for the fever...the tarbardillo which some men have."

Full of the memory of Maguel's dance, it was hard for Diaz to square that brilliance with the small drab man, his body mere sinew girded to bone, as if he had given his substance to the people. Instantly, Diaz prepared himself for what might be a struggle.

His manner reserved, cool, he answered: "Yes, it is typhoid."

Maguel walked to the table overspred with instruments and medications. With slender, finely shaped fingers he took up a scalpel, and delicately with his index finger tried the blade.

"This is good, Médico," he said in his soft sibilant way. "But the blade is not strong. *Inamu*? I should say in your tongue, comprendo?"

The play of words was intended to disparage him, an outsider, and to emphasize that Diaz would always be that. Diaz watched the man replace the scalpel on the tray and then easefully draw a knife from his belt.

"Consider how much better in strength is this blade," Maguel murmured. "And it is good to shave with. *Seka chabo-ara*." He seemed to savor, taste, each Indian word. "See?" He touched the knife softly to his chin, affectionately, his eyes upon Diaz becoming almost caressing. "Or to cut with...or to take out a bullet with."

Diaz became vigilant, though any violence was unthinkable now. There was no threat in Maguel's manner—only an apparently loving attention to the knife. But Diaz realized that the man meant to imply that the bond between him and his knife was not merely surgical— just that much of a warning. Diaz forced himself into the subtle combat.

"You have an excellent weapon." Diaz's voice was suavely cordial. "But this *repiga*...(he pointed to the scalpel...is used only for surgery, for saving lives."

With a shrug, the little mestizo replaced the knife in the case. His eyes scintillated mockery and malice as he said "Some people do not use *knives* to slay with. But I would like to have a *repiga* like yours."

For a time, it seemed to Diaz that no threat at all had been given. The shaman desired such tools, and in a better world this man might have been his peer in medicine. Again, he felt himself drawn to Maguel.

"I would gladly leave the instruments with you when I go," he said.

In the amused malevolence of Maguel's grin he saw his error: his own lie. All this time he had concealed from himself the fact that he must destroy this man! In the summer warmth a chill passed over him.

"Tío is alive and eats well," Maguel stated.

Diaz shifted his position on the stool and meditated a reply, since he must neither bend to the man nor deny him his achievement. He said, "You have saved a man. You have much ability. But I could have healed others who died." He saw that Maguel's stare did not flicker.

"Heal them how, Médico?" Maguel slurred the name. "Healing is a many-headed thing. The *yowami* must bring health to the body, peace to the mind, sanctity to the soul. To heal is to make a man whole!"

Diaz thought: Miaguel had stabbed at the one weakness in Western medicine, and he was reminded of Aristotle's view. In pity, sadness, he searched for a bridge from himself, his world, to Maguel, but there was none.

"I agree with you in principal," Diaz said. "We could learn a great deal from each other." And he saw Maguel's eyes flit pitilessly over him, seeming to comprehend his limbo of feeling.

"To learn is to remember," Maguel said. "What our people see, we try not to forget." He surveyed the glucose and saline bottles on the shelf. "The woman who was to become my mother was found abandoned by your people in one of our fields. She was three months old. One of our hunters saw the rider on horseback who left her there. Your world is fast-turning, and it grinds those inside it and around it. You are the people of the whirlwind!"

Diaz felt the weight of truth in the denunciation. Yet it left out the modus of that cyclone: the freedom and the search.

"You and your people must live within our world," he said bluntly. "In time, there will be no other. I wish only to help you!" He decided to strike with all his force. "You haven't the knowledge to use these tools of mine!"

Maguel's sunless smile darted at him, and he got up and sauntered to the door where he paused.

"You can take them when you leave tonight," Maguel said in his too-quiet voice. "You will leave in the dark. Rojas will help you."

Diaz, hearing the outrageous, flat command, gazed at the little man's face, the jut of the short beard and sardonic mouth. It was less shattering than he expected — a partial relief. All he had to do now was refuse to leave. After that, there was the simple all-absorbing question: would Maguel try to hurt or even kill him?

"Your jefe, Julio, asks me to stay," he said curtly. He saw that the half-caste's profile did not change.

"Julio is a man of thought, not of seeingness," Maguel said. "He is mistaken ... weka-wai. At sundown, go to Rojas' house." He sidled through the door, and where he had stood there was nothing but light.

Diaz lighted a cigarillo, his fingers quivering slightly. He knew that it was fear of himself which swayed him, since he never lied to himself. There was no middleground between Maguel and him, and he himself could not quit; he came from a world where retreat of any kind had become impossible. And his own liberal-humanist creed was not seriously to be doubted. So he was not free to leave, even if he had wished to, and he did not. He was in trouble here; he knew that. It was an emotional trouble, unidentifiable to him. There was something here which he hated and wished to reform, loved and wished to preserve — something that fascinated and horrified him. He understood that any further equivocations could defeat him, that he must proceed without deviation.

He took up the small narrow-necked bottle of mescal which Julio had given him, poured an ounce into a cup and added water. For some reason, he had delayed drinking any of it until now, as if waiting for a time of duress. Holding the cup, he questioned himself. Why drink it at all? What were his real intentions? Did he wish to discover what effect or illusion of power it gave to Maguel? Or could it be that in him was a subconscious hope of receiving some sort of communion with Maguel and his gods and thus averting the clash? He smiled wryly at his self-questionings. No man could weigh his own impulses, divided as man was between his social and individual natures.

He drank half of it at a swallow, like tequila. He could sense it diffusing itself through him downward, and the taste arose — dry, aromatic, acerb with a flavor of the clay from which it sprang. Oddly, he relished it. Was he drinking it just to prove to himself that it was merely a drug or anti-spasmodic which induced mild delusions and schizophrenia, having none of the properties of mana? He finished the cup.

After a time, he returned to the table and poured a second drink. He took it more slowly, awaiting the hallucinogenic buzz, as they termed it in Cambridge. As time passed, he was able to analyze each of the symptoms: a slight ataxia, a tendency to respiratory depression and a slowing of the pulse. No big bang, no grail.

Minutes afterward, a stronger reaction came, an exhilaration in which he saw himself as if from without, from the view of a second persona which edged out of himself. But it was not alarming, and what he saw, as though in the round, was always and singly himself. In him were walls, reefs which no debauchery would ever scale. And though he might by addiction break down the barriers, the euphoria would only crush the modulated, reasoned, and sometimes harmonious organism which was himself.

He wandered through the hut, and far from pleasure he felt a dysphoria unrelated to the look of grave ecstasy on Maguel's face. It was clear that the little shaman's intoxication came mainly from within him. Something lost to the modern psyche no doubt. Still, as a philosophy professor had once remarked to him: "There can be no progress without an equal and concurrent loss." Cynical, but possibly true.

VI

In the later afternoon, two successive messages claimed Diaz's urgent attention: word that Luis Oma's grandmother was dead (he knew that the unknowing ones would affix the blame to him), and word that the hospital shack was in readiness. Acting swiftly in the teeth of Maguel's menace, he took up his valise and hurried outside into the transparent and immaculate day where his shadow itself did not appear. As he walked, a small girl beside a wood-shelter whispered at him just audibly — "*Chabo-chi! Chabo-chi!*"

A pale ectomorph with stringy hair, her gaze followed him up the street. How quickly they pinned the guilt to him! Recalling Rosalina's tears for the old woman, Oma's grandmother, he wondered: how would she truly feel toward *him*?

In a few doorways, women in their bleached skirts, stood stiffly watchful. They seemed to have emerged from the death-haunted houses to feed their sight on the life in the streets. As he crossed the peyote-patio, they regarded him with quiet reproach. Again, their earthy naturalness attracted him. They were not lovely of shape or attire like the sex-pots of Mexico City, but they were graceful and instinctively gay. When they saw him this primeval gaiety dropped from them.

He entered the vacated lodge. Inside, on the scrubbed table was a second Coleman lamp, and on each side of the hut Luis Oma had

made two pallets of skins and blankets, and a fifth in an alcove on
the right side. Beside the entrance were the water samples in
varisized bottles, one of them a Coco-Cola bottle, no doubt found
along the roadside. He took from the case the portable laboratory
and boxes of barbiturates, codeine, and morphine.

When he turned around, he saw her—Rosalina—standing
beside the table. He had not been the least aware of her arrival,
she moved so softly.

"I greet you, Rosalina," he said, his smile easeful, intimate. He
saw: dense dark eyes, outwardly impassive, actually alert and
watchful, a strong body, full breasts lifting and drooping under
the white blouse.

"Julio and my father sent me here," she said in a bright
coloratura tone. "I will do your bidding." Her meekness was like
that of a nun, only less self-conscious.

"You can be of great help," he told her. He placed a stool at the
table for her. "Seat yourself, please."

She perched herself on the stool and folded her hands, her
movements lightsome and smooth. An elegance about her belied
her peon costume, her necklace of cheap tinted stones, the
evidences of dust and grime on her brown naked calves and
ankles.

"What do you ask of me?" She peered up at him, her lips just
suppressing a smile.

Enlivened by her, he began the instructions. "We call this a
hospital. Those who suffer most are brought here. I give orders to
you about each of the patients, as they are called. And you, the
nurse, will please do as I ask."

She listened with extreme care. Then her smile broke out—
sunny and all-encompassing. "Hospital, patients, nurse," she
recited. And her hands pressed deeper between the plumpness of
her thighs.

Diaz was uncertain when the warmth in him became desire. It
just was there, a yearning for her which to him was quite natural,
like the coitus which should be its fulfillment.

"Very good," he said sincerely. "Knowledge comes fast to you." Her smile ended, and her eyes became very sober, dubious. Either she suspected his motives or she might be mindful of Luis Oma's grandmother.

"I am truly sorry about the mother of Luis Oma," he said to her. "When I arrived she was too near to death. Julio knows this."

Rosalina studied him for some time in total silence. Bearing her candid scrutiny, he thought: she would note any lack of frankness. At last, she seemed satisfied.

"Yes," she said. "That is what Luis Oma and I believe." In her voice and lip movements there was a purring songlike femininity that moved him to tenderness and pity while, at the same time, the lower fires of lust spread in his loins. Sweeter because unexpected.

"The patients will arrive soon," he told her. "I am going for them now."

She bowed her head, and with a last glance at her who had brought to him a long-needed flush of enjoyment, he left the shelter.

It was an hour later when, after placing three patients in the clinic under Rosalina's care, Diaz stepped into the coolness of his lodge. He left the door open, and the sunlight, which would reflect any movement, flooded into the room. The night with its hazard drew closer, and the enigma within him persisted. In the midst of treating the patients, the ambivalent feeling rose. Knowing that each of his acts was leading to Maguel's defeat, he had sensed in himself a reluctance to snatch the victory. It was incomprehensible, like his whole attitude to these people. Not an ethnic-tie — that was nonsense!

Checking his supplies, he bent and straightened, and as he did, he glimpsed the shadow in the door. Instantly, Maguel himself shuffled in.

Diaz did not move, struck by the man's visit this long before sundown. Maguel's eyes were just slightly reddened, as from fatigue or drinking.

"I have heard of your 'hospital.'" He spoke sharply. " I can see that you are not ready to leave tonight. Do you need help? *Guiviro si emihe?*" He gave each Indian sound a hissing inflection. "What do you reply to my courteous question, Médico?"

Diaz kept his air of brusque reserve. There could be no physical danger now: if violence came it would be at night, in darkness. Now he must challenge the man, squelch the bluff, if it were that.

"I intend to stay, Maguel," he said. "I took an oath to heal the unwell...so I cannot leave. You understand tnat!"

Maguel's eyes contracted, filling with darkness, before changing into the rueful smile.

"I know that you intend to stay." The carefully moulded, meticulous words. "Not long ago you offered a gift to me." He touched with a fingertip the scalpel. "I have little of worth. So as my gift I have brought this. It is the equal of my own "

He withdrew from inside his black shirt a bone-handled hunting-knife in a deerskin scabbard and laid it on the table.

Diaz contemplated an instant the acute fact of the knife lying there and the gesture behind it. Was it an exchange of mementos, or was it a presentation of a weapon for some unimaginable encounter or duel? He slipped the knife from its casing long enough to examine the six-inch length of pointed honed steel. He re-sheathed the knife.

"I accept your gift," he said with calm formality. "But I must remain here six months to a year."

"No, Médico." Maguel's grin played over him with derisive sadness. "The choice is not yours. You will leave tonight." He accented each syllable. "Do you not guess that I would do or give anything to preserve my people from you? Do you not guess that I, with the help of the gods or without it, will surely exorcize you and the other cabróns from us? Do you not know that I have the power to see who you are...the *chabo-chi*?"

Diaz could feel the outrage, the primitive horror strike against the hardness and ungivingness in himself.

"Do your gods approve of your curses and boasts?" he asked.

Maguel's stare was gleaming-cold, yet half wistful. "What gods do you speak of? You have killed your god!" He added more quietly, "And ours have deserted us!"

Walking toward the light at the door Maguel added, "You are to leave at sundown. Rojas will await you. I bid you be gone!" His last glance at Diaz held a bitterness and rue. Then he disappeared into the dimensionless day.

Diaz stood still for a time, apprizing himself of the truth: that Maguel would come for him or attack him, probably tonight. It appeared to be no bluff—death at Maguel's hand seemed just possible. Awestruck, he pondered it. Death for *him*, a dedicated diagnostician, the end of dreams, projects, achievements! Such things could be. But it altered nothing within him or outside him. His duty lay here, and he could never shirk that. So, in a sense, he had no power to leave or to escape from Maguel.

The knife which Maguel had given him lay before him, as he considered. He well-knew how to defend himself—he must simply guard against the clandestine thrust. After all, he was strong and agile, and the *yowami* a mere shadow. A thrown-knife could catch him off guard, but the Indians regarded that method as beneath them.

Diaz pushed the knife to the far side of the table. He doubted that he needed it or would use it in any case. In the time before nightfall, he must act with speed and certitude to make the hospital fully operable and thereby gain the active allegiance of Julio and the people. He would think about the encounter afterwards.

Seizing his valise, he walked out into the translucent late-afternoon. At that moment, he saw Julio come striding across the corner of the patio—very real yet phantasmal in the brightness. Julio stopped beside him, and the crack in his lens fractured the silver light.

"You have shown power, Médico," Julio stated. "The youths with winged-feet have not undergone the great change to the

bodies of our earth-kin, the coyote and the heron. They live to
breed our race."

With the terror of the night before him, he scanned the *seri-ga-
me*'s face. It was the same — perspicuous, resigned to what
must be — a living-face behind a death-mask.

For an instant, Diaz considered: should he inform Julio of
Maguel's threat? No, it would change nothing really, and it could
lead to catastrophe.

"Thank you for your trust," he said. "I'll do what I can for your
people."

Julio, with his bearing of incredible patience, nodded at him.

"I am tired," Julio said, as if half to himself. "I am not a man of
great faith. But I do what must be done. Sometimes what I hate to
do, I do. I was made for that purpose."

Julio gave a parting signal and walked off with his near-pomp
of carriage and demeanor. Diaz instantly headed for the hospital.

VII

It was six o'clock, and he sat in the makeshift clinic. He had crossed over the tightrope of time allotted to him by Maguel, and progress had been made. Three patients lay along the walls — advanced cases of typhoid, a young woman running high fever and two boys of twelve, sturdy-seeming in their critical stages, a veritable Castor and Pollux of the future, who would survive.

On a stool beside one of them, Rosalina after taking the temperatures was checking pulse rates with a watch, her first acquired skills. He followed the easeful adagios of her movements. She would be with him in this zero-time between the now and the night. Finishing with the boy, she glided to the table and began winding cotton on the sticks, the busy-work he had given her. What were his intentions with her? She was taboo to him, but that might be waived by the tribe. Somehow the thought of miscegenation with her, with her racial oneness, inflamed him further. He thought: was it a suggestion of wrongness in coitus with her that enhanced his longing? The wish to sully her? Another pointless quandary!

Musing, he watched her deft fingers spin the cotton-tips. He believed that it was important to his mission to possess her liking or love. Now that Maguel and he were forever opposed, she assumed a significance: her love for him would betoken success, and a relationship to her as his mistress, if that were allowed,

would amount to intermarriage, the surest means of breaking the
racial shell. It would spell the end of the demon, *Chabo-chi*, and
of tribal segregation.

She began gathering up the cotton swabs. Deeply aroused, his
feelings for her were both lustful and personal, clear and unclear.

"Do you wish to be here with me?" he asked.

She shifted her knees toward him, but her head remained
lowered. "To help a *yowami* is an honor," she said humbly. Her
smile kept its sensuous innocence. "A woman is not often
chosen."

"You honor me too," he said with quiet blandishment' "My
liking for you is very great, Rosalina." Reaching, he gripped her
hand holding the sticks. "Among my people it is called *love*." He
drew his thumb tenderly across the taut ridges of her
knuckles.

She slowly lifted her head and her eyes, direct and unshy,
stabbed into his.

"My liking is as strong as your love." Her voice was quiescent,
demure. "To me, you are like the day-god. The one in the many."

Despite his poise, he was seized by an overmastering joy. He
thought: complete frankness with her would be best — it was their
way and his.

"Listen, Rosalina, if we wished it ... (persuasively but gently he
phrased it) ... could you and I join ourselves together, my body
and yours?" Drawing nearer to her, he curved his arm around her
waist, and placed his hand carefully underneath her breast where
the contour began. "Could we lie together?"

Her mouth kept its upcurl of lubricious innocence. "You are a
yowami," she said. "Your happiness is my rightness." She
laughed briefly, in a deep-throated way. "Would you like to see
me whole? As you do with the patients?"

Nothing could have prepared him for her question. It struck
through his reserve, and he felt himself open up to her in a new
manner. His feelings were changed to a spontaneous sweetness,
drawn from something latent in him.

"If you would like to show yourself to me." He gave her his most vivacious smile.

She rose before him, her shadow thrown against the screen, her rapid fingers unclasping her black sash. Her eyes dwelling on him were sunny and pleasureful as she began to lower the dress over her hips. The transit of the skirt downward and her emerging nudeness took on a sudden meaning beyond themselves. The skirt fell at her ankles, and her hands rising lifted the faded blue blouse and drew it up over her betumbled dark hair. From her feet upward she was entirely exposed. Her arms dropped, and she displayed herself to him without apparent pride or embarrassment.

She stood close to him, her skin earth-tan, the breasts elongated and full, the lower body female but not crude, its clefts and velours not so much naked as clothed in its own nudity. Her form was like any woman's, but to him subtly different. It was she that he saw, not finally her ripe, flawed anatomy.

"Am I good to see?" Her gaze interrogated him.

Reaching, he dropped his hand to the slope of her shoulder. She met his touch, listened to him say — "Yes, the seeing is good." No other comment was needed in the clear, pristine world in which, at least for a moment, she and he existed. Between himself and her otherness was no rift, no blur of abstraction. He might have taken her in his arms, but he became conscious of having heard for some time the coughing and retching of one of the boy patients.

"I must go to him," he told her. "For just one minute."

Leaving her, losing sight of her, did not shatter his elysian mood, the newness within him, He knelt beside the boy and examined him. The boy's lids parted and blinked at him; he was beginning to recover. Later he would administer a tranquilizer. Behind him, he heard her stirring behind the screen, so she must be dressing herself. At that instant, it crossed his mind that she might have been possessed before. Had it really occurred? At one of the festivals when for a few hours the chastity of the people might be discreetly breeched with the consent of all concerned. It was possible. Maguel himself might have been her lover.

He arose, thinking that nothing in his new state of mind or being had altered. But he could tell at once that it had. In that short interlude, he had returned to himself, as the luminous joy had left him. He tried to regain it, and failed. Had the shape of his doubt darkened everything? He hesitated, facing her moving shadow on the screen. He could never return to her again, just as he had been: in that sense he had lost her. He simply confronted the fact and accepted it. Possibly the rapture had been only a form of self-hypnosis.

He stepped behind the screen. Fully dressed, she sat on the stool and flung him her blithe look. Whatever might have changed, his passion for her had not, nor had the pulchritude of her body beneath her clothing.

"Tomorrow night you will come to me," he said intimately. "Is that right, Rosalina?"

Viewing him steadily, she scarcely moved her lips. "Yes, I will come to your *kari-qui*."

Forcing his attention from her he began to prepare the medications. In the meantime the night and whatever it contained which must be vanquished, undone, ended, lay before him.

VIII

He returned to the lodge as the late sunset commenced. From east to west, over the higher and lower mountains, the sky hung in strata of rose and opal. The refracted colors stippled the oblique peaks and glades with softer, related tonalities and hues. Diaz noticed that objects which, in the through-shine of the day were iridescent, had become diaphanous in themselves He entered the dusky stone-house and sat down at the table.

The sheathed knife lay before him, and he took it up and turned it in his hands meditatively. If its purpose had been to dismay him, it had paradoxically armed him against attack. But he questioned whether he could bring himself to slaughter a man unless the death-threat grew very real. He doubted, too, that Maguel would carry out his design. Having lost Julio's support, Maguel was impotent. And surely one so dedicated to his people would hardly risk dishonor and banishment. Still, in the violet depths of the doorway was a potential violence not to be denied.

He traced the top-edge of the blade with his finger, lightly; then the bottom-edge. Both sides of the blade were surgically sharp. It reminded him of the well-known razor that cut both ways. Like Maguel himself. In the light of the present, the shaman was as much a murderer as a healer — and Maguel was far too intelligent not to know that. Then what could his game be? Surely not to deliver his people to death! But one could not be sure — power and pride were basic drives. Whatever the yowami's intentions, he was playing with human lives! It was hard not to detest such a man.

As he re-sheathed the knife, suddenly Maguel's face appeared in his mind's-eye, much too vividly. Annoyed with himself he blinked it away. Could it be that he both admired and abhorred the man more than he consciously admitted? Might the *yowami* represent to him a second self long since rejected? Was it possible that some primitive part of himself welcomed a show-down with the man? He shrugged. How could one feel neutral toward Maguel? But suppose it *did* come to a death-struggle...

After a moment he thrust the knife and case inside his shirt. No danger this early, he reasoned: but later he would bar the door, and tonight certainly he would not sleep.

Nerveless, watchful, he arose and walked outside, behind the hut to the corner of the field. A darker shade passed over him in the abrupt onset of evening, though each gaunt cornstalk held its shape. Everything was visible though veiled, withholding its primal reason for being. No beatitude for him, only the interplay of passion and thought which occasionally produced marvels, sometimes catastrophes. He inhaled from a cigarette as the gradual moonlight came on. From a distant lair up the mountainside a lobo yapped and bayed. It was time for caution. He extinguished the cigarette and walked around the shelter to the door.

It was as he entered the doorway that he either saw or quessed it—a bar of moonlight broken by a shadow or a wisp of sound or nothing at all. But he felt that someone was there, near the window. Maguel was waiting for him.

Diaz remained immobile, a few feet away from what he now supposed was possible death. Moonlight drifted past him, and Maguel's form did not appear or stir. Something worked powerfully at his mind—outrage, fear, loathing—but more than that. He felt in himself instantaneously some point of crucial uncertainty, threatening his whole identity. And the thing—the shadow there—seemed to prey on his uncertainty.

Almost in reflex, he slipped his hand inside his shirt until his palm closed on the hilt of the knife. And he whipped it from the case. Noiselessly, he leaped to the wall opposite to Maguel's concealed form and flattened himself against it. It was then that Maguel's voice floated out of the stillness.

"Diaz...I warned you that if you stayed it would mean death to one of us." Softly inflected, with a caressing cadence, the voice wafted at him, as if disembodied.

He did not answer, could not have spoken. As in every crisis of his life he relied on the precise act. Of that alone could he be certain now. If the man came at him, then he himself would have to strike back. It seemed suddenly that simple.

Diaz waited, as a fine dewy sweat dampened the whole of his body. He sensed, partly heard, the movement as Maguel's black form, crouching low, streaked to the wall at a right angle to him. His pulse stroked faster, harder. It was impossible now not to hate the sinister little man who stalked his very soul. But he was ready. His hand holding the knife merely swung in a half-arc to face the new position of the man. Now, he could speak. "Maguel! If you attack, I must defend my life. Julio will understand."

No answer—just the stalking shadow.

He spoke again. "This trick of yours, *yowami*, does not become a man!" Silence again, and the voice, barely audible: "A man is always becoming something, Diaz. Is it not true?"

For one passing moment, it seemed to Diaz that he could make out dimly the face of the little man in the faint moon-glitter and detect something of the pathetic smile. When Maguel began to move, to take on a shape in the thinning darkness, Diaz simply held the knife at point-thrust position beside him.

The next instant, in total silence, it happened. All he could make out was the whitened form rushing at him— so slight a figure that it appeared almost childlike. Diaz thrust overhand with the blade, and it skimmed along Maguel's shoulder, hardly contacting him. Then, agonized at having missed, he lunged and stabbed the blade straight toward Maguel's naked chest. He felt the knife stick and penetrate the man's rib-cage so deeply that his own fingers clenching the hilt rested against flesh. Flesh that swelled, shuddered, and then fell away.

For a minute afterwards, in his shock, he could hardly connect the sequence of things. Unbalanced by the plunge of the knife, by the fall of Maguel's body which wrested the knife from his hand, he sprawled face-down against the table-top. Immediately, he attempted to straighten himself, but a state of horror paralyzed him. It seemed the longest time before he could remotely connect the self that he had believed himself to be with the one who had struck with a knife. Then, passionately, he found himself standing, hearing the wheeze and sputter of Maguel's breathing, loud in the soundless night. He felt his world and self narrow to a point of nothingness which only his will — clutching to the now, to each emerging moment — could offset.

He lighted the lamp hurriedly and seized a stethoscope. With controlled haste, he dropped to his knees beside the stricken man. He recoiled from the sight: the distortion of the familiar bearded face, the bulge and fixity of the eyes as the mouth gaped for the air that the lungs could not hold. The irreversible change! The knife protruded from the chest at an angle toward the heart, and the blood formed a red swatch from nipple to waistline. Stark, cinematic, it was all quite real, like the gore on an ancestral battleground.

His ear pressed near the wound, he listened to the convulsive cardiac throb. At that moment, a reversal of feeling overtook him — his loathing for the man became pity and grief, just as his role, his identity, had changed from killer to doctor. He thought of the unfathomable waste.

It was then that Maguel began to speak, just higher than a murmur, the lax lips barely moving.

"You have killed me, man!... it was God-willed." A pause, a harsh suspiration, and the voice went on, precise and faint. "These people... are yours." A calmness underlay the tone and face.

By the time Diaz fixed the lobes of the stethoscope to his ears, Maguel had ceased to breathe. And as Diaz listened, the heart, after a tentative flutter, became still.

His hand holding the scope fell. A revulsion for his own act — a wish to cancel or disown it — shook his mind. Yet he was himself again, able to detach his larger purpose from contingent evils, including this one of death. All choice was, in a degree, evil. One must accept the cost — and the body before him might have been his own! Defending himself, he had killed a man — an appalling fact, but one with which he must cope. He had killed a man who, in another age, might have become great, but who, in terms of the present, was his people's worst enemy. Thus he, Ramón Diaz, had killed one man — the shadow of a man — so as to spare the lives of many. He did not doubt that the people, however they might grieve, would finally accept the truth.

Still, as he crouched there, a horror persisted which partly outran his reason and convictions. Gradually, he became aware of something overlooked or missing: Maguel's knife.

Quickly, he groped over and under the man, and found nothing. Rising, he took up a flashlight and shone it around the room, over the whole interior. The knife was not visible, was not in fact there!

Diaz weighed the enormity of it. It could not be that Maguel had sacrificed himself, had staged his own murder, so as to discredit him. An unbelieveable melodrama! And yet it must be so. Maguel's zeal was of that pitch, and this act had been his last fanatic gamble. Was it possible that, through this subterfuge, Maguel might defeat him? Diaz could not be certain. He knew that he must forego all speculation, and seek through his own truth and convincingness to undo Maguel's grim masterwork.

With cold intentness, he took up the small body, light as a schoolboy's, and laid it across the table. Bending over the dead man he carefully removed the knife from the clotted wound, leaving a clean incision in the bronze skin. With the same care he wrapped the blade in gauze and began cleansing the blood from the chest, using a sponge dipped in alcohol. The dead face seemed to muse or meditate timelessly under his temporal care. With the lids of the eyes partly closed and the mouth awry under the grotesque beard, the face took on a cast both benign and hobgoblin. It matched his own torn and contrary feelings about the man.

He was drying the body with a towel when he heard soft footfalls. Straightening, he saw Luis Oma standing just outside the door. Diaz realized that his future here hinged on this minute.

"I come to ask if Maguel is here," Luis Oma said. And looking around, he saw the body on the table.

Diaz did not speak as Oma, after a brief hesitation, came and stared downward at Maguel's body. Oma's expression did not alter visibly in its masculine gentleness and candor. It was, as if he came forewarned, or possibly he had passed beyond astonishment.

"He is dead," Diaz said to him. "I am truly sorry."

Luis Oma turned and appraised him.

"How did you kill him, Médico?"

Diaz met the man's eyes with his own blunt frankness. "He hid in the dark of the hut, and he rushed at me. I defended myself. Afterwards, I found that he carried no knife." Oma's glance showed a sadness, all the greater for its tranquility.

"I understand," he answered.

"A truth is of a wholeness." The wire of tension snapped for Diaz. Oma believed him, and Maguel's suicidal design had crumbled. He watched as Luis Oma bent over the corpse. He was not prepared for Luis Oma's abrupt exclamation.

"Maguel...I grieve for you!" The cry became shrill, ululant. "Maguel, you have not failed us!" Then the mellifluous Indian words—"Nehe emihe-niwara huku...I am yours."

Diaz could not guess the exact meaning of the outcry, apart from its devotedness. He crossed to Oma's side and placed his hand on the young man's shoulder.

"To Maguel, it was the will of the gods," he said to Oma. "Can you tell me why?"

Oma's answering gaze was direct and mild, but with a suggestion of a distance between them.

"This evening he told me that his hate for you had ended," Oma stated. "Within himself, he was not a man of hate."

It was as if a corner of the truth was swept bare—enough for Diaz to glean the rest, though not to think it through. The flicker of lamp-light between the two figures subtly united them in a nexus of flame.

"The mourners and the bearers will come soon," Oma said.

Luis Oma passed him, the lacey sombrero strung over his shoulders, and stepped into the moonlight.

Diaz, left beside the corpse, drew it all together in his mind. Maguel had sought neither to kill him nor to strip him of his power—that was plain. Too late, Diaz saw in the shaman the adversary of death in all its modes. But Maguel had known that only through his own death could he will over to his people some portion of a possible future in an alien world to which he himself could not belong. How carefully Maguel had plotted it, from the gift of the knife until this moment.

His attention was driven to the quiet body on the table. It seemed to live on, evoking again his own hate and fascination, his self-doubts, his own throbbing blood-lust. He surmised that nothing in himself had escaped Luis Oma's scrutiny. That accounted for Oma's remoteness, which would reappear in all the others, Rosalina among them. They would accept him as the médico, but they could not love him, not because he represented the evil one, but because he was unworthy of love. To them he must remain at best a guide to limbo. Yes, the truth was of a wholeness.

Bending, he drew a blanket over the small body, just as on some latter day another impersonal hand would draw over him or his successors a similar shroud.

On his way to the door he heard the chant begin. Not lively or urgent like the *rutuburi*, it was a slow threnody without rattles or harmony.

From the doorway, Diaz could plainly see the procession forming on the patio as two men at the forefront waved their funeral flambeaux. Immediately, the column began to wind toward his lodge, Julio in the lead, then Luis Oma who wore the ruff of aigrette. The flames and smoke blent with the marine-blue of the greater night, and at moments the faces themselves verged on nothingness. Other fires were burning in the shelters, and the breeze was once again altogether sweet with cedar as it had been generations past in the era before *Chabo-chi*.

THE AXING OF LEO WHITE HAT
By Raymond Abbott

To
O.B. Thomas, Jr.

1

On the day government checks are supposed to come to Cut Meat a lot of men usually congregate in front of Goodwin's Market or wait inside the tiny Cut Meat post office hoping that when the postmistress opens her window she'll hand over a check. Anyone who doesn't get a check on the day it's due is sure the white postmistress is holding it back. Though no one can prove it, many in the village suspect she regularly delays checks, when check day comes on a Friday or Saturday, to avoid a weekend of drunken brawling and trouble.

The Indians on the steps to the post office just talk quietly among themselves, waiting patiently for the window to open. If all the mail that came in from Alliance that morning were given out, and if the sack contained veteran's checks, there would be a lot of cutting up and partying in Vetal and Crockston and other off-reservation towns

There was a big man who towered over everyone there. Ben Whipple was a breed. In striking contrast to the Indians around him, he was talkative and very sure of himself. He smiled and waved his hands as he spoke and would flash a smile when he saw someone he knew. His few teeth were white, some he'd lost in rodeo riding, others in fights. He had a slightly crippled left hand, another souvenir from a rodeo accident, though he used it as if nothing were wrong. His light brown eyes, were cold, vicious and penetrating.

Everyone in Cut Meat knew Whipple to be a cruel, murdering son of a bitch, especially when he was drunk. He would lie, cheat and steal from anyone, even his own family. Everyone knew about the men he had beaten senseless in drunken brawls. Lyle Horse Looking was found dead in the brush miles from town with eight stab wounds in his back. He was last seen riding in a car with Ben and five or six others, all drunk and acting wild. Many townsfolk were sure Ben had done the killing, but when the reservation police chief, a white man (a little Indian blood), brought him in for routine questioning, Ben said he couldn't have done it, as he and Lyle Horse Looking were almost brothers, having grown up together, and he even hinted somewhat coyly that Charlie Crazy Cat, who was also in the car, had a pretty damn good reason to kill Horse Looking seeing as the Horse Lookings and Crazy Cats had been fueding for years and everyone in town knew it. He didn't come out and accuse Charlie, but it wasn't long before the police chief came looking for Crazy Cat with a warrant for his arrest for the murder of Lyle Horse Looking. Somehow Crazy Cat found out what was going on and fled town, riding out on the prairie on horseback just as the police pulled up to his father's shack down back near the creek.

2

Some people moved for the door of the post office, the window was finally opening. Whipple said to Eagle Man, "That goddam bastard of a white woman better give you your check this morning, or else I'll go in after her myself. I've got a mighty big thirst building,"

Eagle Man walked in and got his veterans' check. Five or six other checks came too, checks that had gotten held up (belonging to those thought likely to cause trouble), but had now mysteriously found their way to the correct post office. The postmaster of Alliance received a call from the state capitol at Pierre concerning another complaint about mail getting held up. He knew and approved of the way money was sometimes held back. But after the call from Pierre he ordered all checks given out.

If the money had only gotten delayed somehow...

But life is not like that on the reservation; if one weekend is quiet and accident-free, the next promises to be filled with violence and death.

It's the boredom that does it, some say. And the liquor. The liquor hardly ever kills by destroying the liver or pancreas. It doesn't have time on a reservation. More often, the drinking causes the most God-awful automobile accidents or the fiercest, bloodiest fights, or whatever else happens when the ferocity of one man out of his mind from too much alcohol is pitted against another.

3

By three p.m. that day three or four parties were going at full gait. One was at the Eagle Man's, another next door at the Shots' house, and one at the Little Crow place across the roadway. And in a little log house off by itself the Black Bears were at it. They didn't get any government money, but the two eldest boys had done a couple of day's ranch work for a white operator. They had drawn their pay the night before and everyone was drunk except for the ten-year-old. He usually stayed away when things got bad, sometimes visiting with the missionary lady, Liz.

The longest drinking bout, a marathon lasting a month, was under way at the White Hats' place, a small wood frame house on the north edge of the village. The green paint was fresh and bright on the small building, and next to the other shanties it looked better kept, a little like a trim lake or seashore cottage. But it was, in fact, just like the others in town: run down inside, uninsulated, without plumbing, two or three rooms with a woodburning stove. White Hat himself was not very well. He had arthritis, was blind in one eye, and was gradually losing the sight in the other. He walked with a limp because of a gun shot wound. He was unable to work most of the time, not that there was much work anyway, but he was able to get along much better than most in town because he had lots of reservation land and received lease payments from white cattle operators who ran cattle on his sections. His wife and he held long drinking bouts — affairs that even the heaviest drinkers in town left after a week.

The White Hats had a son about twenty-two years old who sometimes lived with them. He was already almost hopelessly alcoholic, although sometimes he got away to do ranch work off the reservation. He could remain sober then. But he always came back and resumed the old life again, like his father before him.

4

Ben Whipple was very drunk by the time night came, as were the Eagle Mans, the Shots, the Little Crows, and two or three other families in town. They all lived together not far from the creek. Whipple announced in drunken slurs that it was time to go somewhere else, since the liquor was pretty much used up and Eagle Man's check was mostly spent. So Whipple, Eagle Man, Jimmy Little Crow and Tuffy Bordeaux climbed in Harry Shot's beige Chevrolet and drove off. Harry Shot was behind the wheel, drunk and grinning. Tuffy, once settled in the back seat, could still hear voices and feel the jolts and bangs as the car raced down the narrow gutted road at the rear edge of the village. After a few moments Tuffy heard nothing; he had passed into a deep drunken sleep.

After a few hundred yards, Whipple hollered for Shot to stop in front of White Hat's place. Whipple got out and waved Shot on, "Go get Lilly and some other cunts." He walked toward White Hat's little green shack a few yards from the road.

"I'm gonna get some more beer — they ought to have some left. Come back and get me in a few minutes."

Shot drove away, leaving Whipple at the edge of the barbed wire gate that surrounded the little plot of land where the house stood. Whipple entered through the gate opening and called out to White Hat, "You in there, Leo?" White Hat hadn't forgotten for a moment the beating Whipple had layed on his son a few months before. The boy was still hurting. White Hat went to the door and yelled, "You son of a whore, get the fuck off my property." But Whipple didn't seem bothered; he just grinned and tried to calm White Hat, thinking of the liquor or money he might get from him if he could just talk a few minutes. But White Hat was having none of it. He cursed again, then picked up a rock and hurled it in Whipple's direction. Whipple didn't move fast enough, and the rock caught him square in the back, right between the shoulder blades. The force of the rock wasn't great enough to hurt him, but half drunk as he was, his anger rose and the grin disappeared. He started for the gate, cursing and muttering and getting angrier by the minute. For a moment he stopped at the barbed wire fence next to a woodpile to light a cigarette. He spotted an ax lying on the ground beside the cuts of wood. He took the ax in hand and with no hesitation started back toward the little cabin. White Hat had already gone back in and the door was closed and all seemed quiet. Whipple didn't know who was in there with Leo. He banged hard on the door and stepped way back into the darkness as he heard White Hat shuffle up to the door.

"What do you want? I told you before..." White Hat began, stepping out of the lighted doorway into the darkness and cold night air. He couldn't see Whipple, and Whipple, not knowing or caring whether he saw him or not, without a word of warning, brought the ax from behind his back and let it fly sidearm with the full strength of his thick arms and shoulders, catching White Hat just to the right of his neck. The force of the blow was so great it threw him four or five yards away into a heap next to some bags of beer cans that had been placed outside the cabin walls.

White Hat didn't cry out. There was only the thud of the ax and the crash as he hit the beer cans and the wall of the cabin. But once on the ground he gave out a loud groan that grew into a piercing wail as the pain reached him at last through the shock.

That sound coming from White Hat sent Whipple scurrying away, frightened and suddenly sober. His anger disappeared at that moment as a panic developed within him with the realization of what he had done and the trouble he could be in. He ran for a few yards up the road where he saw Harry Shot's car loaded with people, a couple of them women, coming for him. He waved at Shot and jumped into the back seat as the car slowed. Once in, Harry stepped down hard on the gas and the car sped away, fish-tailing along the little road and barely missing a dog that was in the way. At the junction near the market Shot turned left onto the new gravel road that led to the state highway junction where the oil surfaced road began.

5

As Harry Shot sped along the road he shook his head trying to clear it while the car fish-tailed, this time barely missing the deep grass-covered culvert on either side of the road. He didn't want to hit the culverts again — he did that once before and had broken an axle and couldn't get the car out for a week.

Beside him was Clorine Broken Lance almost passed out drunk hanging on him and making the driving and concentration harder. He pushed her into Jimmie Little Crow, the hunchback, who was sipping from a bottle of cheap gin.

In the back seat Lilly Blue Thunder, a white-looking half breed woman of about twenty-two, Eagle Man and Whipple were passing around a bottle of gin, laughing and carrying on. Tuffy was still passed out in the corner. Lilly was beginning to feel the liquor, as Whipple and Eagle Man kept giving her the gin — helping her along.

Harry Shot slowed the car at the junction and crossed the state road, heading for Redridge. There was a spirit of revelry and high feeling in the car. Ben Whipple didn't think or worry like other men. He was more inclined to figure that by morning things would be straightened out somehow. The reservation police had never bothered him much in the past.

6

White Hat's son found his father bleeding and near death at the cabin door. The boy was so drunk he didn't hear the commotion at first, but at last he was awakened by the screams and groans coming from outside. No one else was in the cabin, except his mother who was uselessly passed out drunk. Elmer White Lance and his common-law wife had left a half hour before — they crawled away, they were so drunk. When he saw his father, he had no notion of what had happened, only that he was badly hurt.

Drunk and stumbling through the darkness, the junior White Hat made his way as fast as he could across the gravel road up to Father Keel's place.

Father Keel was the community's priest, a member of the reservation's Jesuit order. He was obsessed with finding the bones of Crazy Horse. Every chance he had, he went to the Badlands west of the reservation searching for the gravesite. And when he returned, he was even more hopeful than before he left. He would tell anyone who would listen how close he was to finding the burial site. The Sioux who had carried the dead leader to the Badlands after he was murdered had not wanted the grave marked or known. But this seemed of no importance to the priest. He persisted in his quest year in and year out, moving around the Badlands, ever expecting to find the grave over the next rock formation.

Jimmy White Hat came up to the steps of the house, rang a bell that played a tune he had never heard before. It was a French religious hymn. An elderly Indian woman dressed in a long, navy-blue dress answered the door. When she saw White Hat and took note that he had been drinking, she immediately thought he had come to borrow money from the good father, as so many others in town frequently did. She tried to save the priest the inconvenience of this interruption by telling the visitor the good Father was away.

White Hat didn't believe her and screamed at the woman. He was so loud that Father Keel, who was downstairs in the recreation room preparing his regular Sunday sermon, heard the commotion and came up. As soon as he heard the story from White Hat, muddled as it was, he grabbed his little black bag that contained the oils and other preparations he would need for administering the last sacrament, and with White Hat went directly to the cabin where his father lay moaning and half dead.

7

The cheap gin tasted good to Tuffy as he took a gulp too long to please Whipple. Whipple, sitting next to him, pulled the bottle away roughly when he saw Tuffy held it too long.

"You fucka, we ain't got so much to have you drinking that way," he said. He handed the bottle to Lilly sitting next to him. She drank a little and handed it back, looking a little sick. By this time she was very drunk and was having trouble holding up her head.

Tuffy watched her for a minute, thinking she sure looked like a white girl, not much Indian blood in her.

He tried to sit up a little and peer out the side window into the darkness. He could barely make out the barbed wire fence on the edge of the gravel road—barbed wire to keep the stock from wandering onto the highway. All he could see was the blur of objects whizzing by as he tried to focus his eyes on the outline of the poles.

"That goddam Shot must be doing a hundred," he thought before passing out again and leaning against Whipple.

Whipple was trying to undress Lilly. He pushed Tuffy out of the way.

As Tuffy lay in the corner not knowing what was going on, Harry Shot forced a pickup truck coming in the opposite direction to detour into a ditch. The other driver who was from the

reservation, wanted little to do with a car whose lights came at
him first from one side of the road and then the other, and needed
no explanation of what was going on.

Shot was on the Crockston road headed for Nebraska, having
made the turnoff beyond Redridge Community. The road was
gravelled and wide but the car continued to zig-zag as Shot shook
his head in an effort to see better. Several times he just missed
going off into a ditch. There was little traffic on the road that night
as they headed south to Cody, Nebraska, a little town a few miles
west of Crockston. Until *My Brothers Place* burned down it was
the favorite drinking spot of reservation Indians. Most white
folks didn't miss it very much, with all the trouble it brought in
the form of drunk Indians every weekend, or whenever they
got a little money. Now most Indians went to Cody or some
other town in Nebraska.

"Christ sake, drive straight," Whipple bellowed as the car
continued to weave down the highway, seeming less in control
with every swerve. Whipple had Lilly completely undressed and
propped up against the seat in the corner. With Eagle Man next to
him and Tuffy in the other corner he didn't have much room. Lilly
was still conscious and aware of what was happening, but could
do nothing to stop it—not that stopping him was in her mind so
much as the crowdedness of the car and the discomfort she was
feeling. Whipple, his pants down around his ankles, mounted her
as best he could in the crowded car, his full weight coming to rest
on top of her. As he got settled in her and began to move rapidly
he wanted more room. By this time Eagle Man had shoved up
against Tuffy hard as he could. But he found even more room as
Whipple swung wildly with his right hand, barely missing Eagle
Man's head.

Whipple lay back and sighed loudly after finishing. Lilly
passed out, but her head jerked slightly as she spit up the gin she
was drinking. Nobody noticed.

With all his pushing Whipple woke Tuffy, who now sat up. As
Tuffy tried to figure just where he was, Eagle Man was telling one
of his many yarns, about a coyote that followed him nearly one

whole night in a snowstorm. It was February, he said, and he was walking on the road to Mission Town from Valentine, Nebraska, after having been dumped midway between the two towns by several Pine Ridge Sioux who thought it would be funny to leave him miles from nowhere. There was no great love between his tribe and the Oglala or Pine Ridge Sioux. He told how that coyote just kept a safe distance waiting for him to slip and fall or get numb from the cold. But it didn't happen — he said the obvious — and he ended the story with a laugh and took a long slug from the nearly empty bottle of gin.

"I just outwalked the critter, but he weren't no bad coyote, no sir, he was just doing what he was taught when he got hungry — just like I'd done had I been born a coyote. Sometimes I get to wondering if that coyote got much to eat that winter. It was a rough one, that I remember."

Tuffy saw lights up ahead — really, only one, a large overhead streetlight that lit the entire center of a little town, which had only three buildings — a garage, a general store, and a barn. They passed some railroad tracks without slowing very much and the car jolted and swerved to the right as they hit. Somehow Shot kept it on the road. Off to the left of the tracks a couple of hundred feet stood a raised wooden platform shed. It was a dull yellow in color, the result of years of neglect by the railroad and the constant punishment of prairie weather. A sign hung out over the tracks. It, too, was faded, and the letters were barely readable. A light set over the sign illuminated the lettering and Tuffy saw it as they sped off beyond the tracks turning right at the intersection in the direction of Cody, four or five miles west on Nebraska Route 18. Tuffy recognized the word on the sign — *Crockston.*

8

To the tourist, Cody, Nebraska is little more than a gas or coffee stop along the straight stretch of highway that runs east and west across Nebraska. The town lies about 200 feet north of Route 18, and not far from the railroad tracks that run almost parallel to the road. The town is encircled by a grove of trees, a kind not commonly seen on dry prairie lands. Some say that the trees were brought west by early white settlers and planted to provide shade from the hot summer sun. When carefully watered and cared for, they grow well even in dry times. Others say the trees were planted during the WPA days of the Depression.

From the highway the trees help to hide the town from view so that a traveler has to turn off the highway and drive across the railroad tracks to see that a town lies in that patch of woods. But it isn't a very big town (no more than 220 people at most). But then there aren't very many big towns in Nebraska west of Omaha. And on a hot summer day if the temperature were near 100°, that clump of trees would look mightly inviting to the hot and weary traveler driving along Route 18.

To the reservation Indian, however, Cody, Nebraska is an altogether different attraction. It's the closest off-reservation drinking spot since *My Brothers Place* in nearby Crockston closed down. On weekends drunk Indians frequently wander the narrow streets of Cody going in and out of the two cafe-bars that provide the income for about four or five white citizens. On a good weekend, that is, when checks come to the reservation or lease money is paid out by the Bureau of Indian Affairs (on behalf of white ranchers), the two bars are full of Indians. And the sound of loud country or rock music disturbs the quiet of a small Nebraska town.

Harry Shot, Ben Whipple and the others pulled into Cody. Already the town was full of Indians from Redridge Reservation in South Dakota.

Of the two bars in town one had a faded sign that read only "Cafe," while the other had no sign at all. Inside the second place, there were several wooden booths pushed against a wall. On the opposite wall extending about halfway to the back of the building was a narrow bar where the patrons stood. There were no seats. The bar ended at a wall that separated the bar from the dance floor. Around the sawdust-covered dance floor, were some tables, chairs, and a band, the *Brass Rings*, three reservation Indians with slick hair combed back in the style of the 1950's.

Whipple, looking more sober than the others, led in the group from the reservation. He nodded to several friends he recognized and started for the back part where the band and tables were located.

The barkeeper saw him come in and grew nervous when he thought of how many times the son of a bitch Whipple had broken up barrooms all over the territory — from Sioux Falls to Bismarck, North Dakota. There wasn't a saloon keeper that did business with Indians on a regular basis that hadn't at least heard stories about Ben Whipple. And most had had dealings with him at one time or another. A Sioux Falls proprietor told a story of how one time Whipple got released from jail on a Saturday afternoon in Sioux Falls and headed immediately for a beer; he found himself in jail a week later in Billings, Montana with a piece of his ear cut off and no recollection of what happened that week. A man with Whipple's kind of reputation was someone who needed watching, the barkeeper decided, fingering the shotgun he kept under the bar.

Whipple took a table and sat down with the others and yelled to the barkeeper to bring a round of drinks. Eagle Man had just enough of his veterans' check to cover them.

The *Brass Rings* were loud and switched from rock to country and western. They played tunes like Buck Owen's "Sam's Place" and a slow, sad song by David Houston called "Almost Persuaded."

The dancers—almost all of them Indians, although there were a few local cowboys and ranchers—jumped around on the floor, some so drunk they hardly noticed the music. A few had all they could do to keep from falling down as they attempted to keep up with the faster songs.

The clock on the wall behind the bar said 11:30, but it was only 10:30. The bar closed at 1:00 a.m. Mountain Time, but on a busy weekend it took every bit of that extra hour to get the Indians out.

At the table sat Whipple, Tuffy and Lilly; Clorine sat next to Harry Shot leaning against his shoulder, her arm locked in his. Jimmy Little Crow stood next to Harry as they all listened to Eagle Man tell about a trip to the Sitting Bull Stampede in Mobridge, South Dakota one Fourth of July. When his wife first saw the lights of Mobridge after driving for fifty miles over the darkened prairie, she began to cry. He said she always started to cry whenever they got too far from the reservation. He thought the part about his wife crying was the silliest thing anyone could do with the lights of the city ahead and all kinds of fun waiting for them.

"We was driving along the road—it was dark and there was no lights and then we saw the lights of Mobridge. She was quiet and attending to the children and all of a sudden she just starts crying. Mobridge ain't no big town, but at night those lights shine like the Chicago skyline, and when she says, 'I want to go home,' I comfort her best way I can, but I sure ain't going home. Anyhow, I knew she would be all right once we got into town and had a couple of beers in the Cowboy Bar, but it sure gets hard when you have the little ones to carry around with you."

Whipple was noticing a woman across the room and hadn't listened to the last part of Eagle Man's story. Then, Clorine, drunk out of her mind, got up and started screaming and shaking. The band stopped playing and the place was quiet as the barkeeper moved slowly and cautiously, expecting the worst, toward the table. He saw the girl clearly for the first time and guessed she was under age, which could mean much trouble if he didn't get her quiet and out of his place. But when he saw Whipple look up at the screaming girl and seem about to take control of the situation, he stopped, deciding maybe he ought to hold back a minute. Like everyone else he just watched to see what would happen next. He didn't have to wait very long as a heavy beer mug was thrown from where the band was playing. It hit Clorine in the center of her face with a thud, bounced off, and shattered on the floor. She fell over to the sawdust floor, her face bleeding and contorted in a grimace of pain until she passed out. The beer and gin she had been drinking all night seemed to have done little to deaden the pain.

Whipple sat for a moment then picked up the chair he had been sitting in. In one hand, he carried it, like a switch, swinging the chair overhead wildly. The band ran as he went behind the bandstand to a table where three Indians, two men and a woman, sat. Without saying a word, Whipple swung the chair at shoulder height, hitting the woman and one man in the first swing and throwing them sprawling onto the dance floor. No one moved to help them—even the barkeeper kept away, figuring the fight would be over when Whipple finished.

The remaining Indian, the one Whipple guessed threw the mug, stood facing him, recognizing him for the first time and deciding it was no good to beg for mercy. Although frightened, the man looked as if he might try to fight back and this willingness to defend himself made Whipple even angrier. But there was no fight; Whipple with one very fast kicking motion brought up his right leg, catching the man aside of the head with a heavy boot, the force of which knocked him unconscious immediately. Whipple then walked over to where the man lay sprawled on the floor and kicked him. Every man in the bar turned away rather than witness the blows that were layed on the unconscious man. It was more like he was kicking a sack full of rags than a man.

Finally the barkeeper's lowered and cocked shotgun intervened. He ordered Whipple and the others with him to get out. After picking up Clorine from the floor, they departed. All the time the barkeeper kept the gun pointed at Whipple, hoping he wouldn't have to shoot. His hands shook as he followed them out the door with the barrel of his shotgun. As the trouble lessened the barkeeper was even more nervous, glad he didn't have to shoot someone.

Whipple, Eagle Man, Tuffy and the others left the Cody bar and sat in Shot's car for an hour or more drinking the beer that Jimmy Little Crow had bought at the other bar. It was past midnight before they left Cody for the drive back to the reservation. Harry Shot still drove. Clorine sat next to him, her face bleeding less now. As she leaned against Shot's shoulder, she slept fitfully, sobbing quietly every few minutes. In the back seat Whipple, getting drunker from the beer and little gin there was left, bragged about what he had done.

Not far out of Cody they came on a car that was stalled. Five persons were standing in the cold beside it. All were Indians, drunk and oblivious to the cold. They were wearing light shirts without jackets and seemed confused as to why their car wouldn't go anymore. A woman was standing outside drunk, with an infant in her arms. She looked as if she might at any moment drop the baby on the hard road. Shot slowed as he approached and decided to stop, because it was such a cold night.

But as Shot slowed down Whipple looked up from the seat and hollered at Shot, "What the fuck are you doing—get the hell going! Them fools probably run that thing out of gas. They'll only want to drink our beer."

Shot stepped on the gas and sped around the stalled car, leaving the woman with the baby and the men staggering in a drunken stupor. They didn't notice that a car had just passed, leaving them to sit until someone came around in the morning.

It took Shot more than an hour to drive the forty miles to the Cut Meat village junction. Meanwhile, his driving got worse. At one point Whipple, Eagle Man and Tuffy had to get out of the car and help push it from a ditch. Whipple cursed Shot the entire way after that.

Cut Meat village was three miles in from the junction over a gravel road. It was a clear night — a star-filled night. Radiational cooling sent the temperature down to below zero. From the junction turnoff the bright lights in the center of the village were visible. They were the only lights on the darkened prairie. Shot drove down the gravel road, stirring up dustclouds as he went along. Inside the car the drinking, laughing, and yelling went on as before.

Shot drove through the center of the village by the post office, the grocery store, and the town's one gas station. There was no one in the streets, no activity of any kind; only the silence of 2 o'clock on a Sunday morning and the crackling, humming sounds of the lights overhead. The lights had been installed by the BIA two years before. In a village where more than half the houses weren't wired for electricity, the lights seemed to be out of place, put there by mistake. It was as though in all their brightness they should be lighting the city streets in Cleveland instead of spreading their strong beam over a little shantytown in the middle of the prairie that had no reason to want its ugliness and squalor advertised like an illuminated billboard.

After driving through the empty town Whipple decided they should continue west to the crossroads and then take the road to Vetal, another off-reservation drinking spot in the next county.

Tuffy had sobered up some and, feeling tired and a little sick, wanted to get out. Shot stopped the car outside the village on the west side just beyond the gray adobe church — the Roman Catholic Church that belonged to Father Keel. It was very dark. The red tailights of Shot's car grew dimmer as Shot and the others drove west toward Vetal.

The road underfoot was rocky, and Tuffy stumbled over some of the larger stones as he groped around in the darkness. He walked up a little hill toward the bright lights in the center of the village. He wobbled along a gully which in the spring usually was washed out with the first heavy rainfall.

Tuffy was still a little drunk and headed for his house to sleep off the effects of the beer and gin.

Tuffy stopped on top of the hill in front of Father Keel's little adobe church. The churchyard was dark except for the light from a 40-watt bulb in a fixture that hung on the side of the church. Tuffy stood in the dim light near the church entrance for a moment. He decided to go to his grandfather's house rather than chance going home and finding his mother drunk and belligerent as she usually was by this time of night. His grandfather had a three-room shack, large by comparison with other houses in the village, but flimsy. The thin clapboards were gray and worn from the constant wind and the alternating bitter cold and scorching heat of winter and summer.

The floors in the house were dirt, and the heat came from a wood stove. It was often crowded there, but Tuffy liked staying with his grandfather because there was almost never any fighting. Grandpa Bordeaux didn't allow any drinking, and whenever an argument developed, as it occasionally did, those involved were asked to leave. While Grandpa Bordeaux was an old man, and certainly not able to force troublemakers to leave, he usually got his way. Everyone respected his wishes. Drunks never came around unless they were ready to go to bed and sleep it off. Tuffy and a lot of others who needed a place to sleep were welcome there. There always seemed to be a lot of people in the little house, at least for the five years since Grandpa Bordeaux' wife died. He seemed to like having a lot of people around, especially his grandchildren, Tuffy in particular.

"Tuffy's a good boy" he would say. "He's got a warm generous way about him, but he's seen so much trouble in his short life. It don't hardly seem right a boy like him should have so much grief. His father's gone and probably dead, and his poor mother all the time drunk and nasty to him, abusing that boy something awful.

It's a wonder he ain't turned out real mean. He's done real well,
Tuffy, real well."

Tuffy decided to take the shortcut to his grandfather's place by
walking through the churchyard. He stumbled over the low
barbed wire fence that encircled the little Catholic cemetery
behind the church where his little sister was buried. She, like so
may others, had been killed in a car wreck.

Crossing the cemetery, Tuffy came out behind Grandpa
Bordeaux' cabin and was about to go around front to the entrance
when he saw a light shining from Sister Elizabeth's house. There
were no other lights on in town and Tuffy wondered what Liz
could be doing up at this time of the morning. Feeling a lot less
tired after walking in the cold night air, he decided to visit her. He
knew she didn't object to a late caller, apparently not caring any
longer that the town gossips had her sleeping with half the men
who stumbled up to her door drunk. It wasn't true, she would say,
and she didn't intend to have gossipy women dictating her life.
She knew she ought to be a bit more discreet for the sake of
propriety, if not for some other more important reason, such as
her own personal safety. But for Liz, her own safety was not an
issue. It never once entered her mind that she might get hurt. As
long as Liz had been in Cut Meat no one seemed to cause her any
trouble, except maybe to borrow a little money, which she never
got back and never expected to. Wherever Liz went, she struck
people the same way: crazy, yet almost saintly.

When Tuffy got to Liz's door he didn't hear any noise inside.
Tuffy walked in the door and tripped over a large aluminum
wash tub left in the shadow. As he moved toward the kitchen of
the little cabin he cursed Liz for leaving the tub where somebody
could trip over it in dark.

"Where have you been, Tuffy?"

"Why'd ya leave that damn tub there," he muttered. "Got some
coffee?" He walked over to the stove in the corner near the
window. He hoped she wouldn't go on with whatever she was
about to say.

"You know the police were here a while ago?" she said. Tuffy twisted the knob on the gas stove trying to get some fire under the coffee pot. He seemed to be paying no attention to what she was saying.

"Someone near killed Leo White Hat with an ax." "Cut him up terrible so that even Father Keel was called down to his house to give him the last rites of the church. The tribal police are looking for whoever done it, and they were asking about you, Tuffy Bordeaux. They want to know where you were, and so do I."

Tuffy blandly took in the tale of the axing of White Hat. He wasn't much shocked at the news, since violence and killing in Cut Meat and just about every other town on the reservation were something he had grown up with. It was nothing new, but when Liz connected his name to what happened he looked up with a genuinely puzzled look on his face.

"Me?" he said, then grinning, "Shit, you got to be kidding. I was riding with Harry Shot, Eagle Man, Ben Whipple and some others. We went to Crockston and Cody. I don't know nothing about any axing—they'll tell you where I was."

"All the same, Tuffy, the police are looking for you. They think you know something about it or else why'd they want to see you? Huh, Tuffy?"

"Well, I don't know nothing about no axing of White Hat," Tuffy repeated, loud and angrily. He threw down his metal coffee cup half full of coffee and walked toward the door to leave. He wanted to blame Liz for all of this and began to curse her again.

"You fat fucka, you don't know shit!"

"Don't talk to me that way, Tuffy," she said. "You better get out of here." She pointed to the door behind where he was standing. "The police may find you here and involve me in your doings." It was a parting remark she knew would make him angry, even though she didn't really think Tuffy had done the axing.

"I told you, you white son-of-a-bitch, I never done anything, and you better stop saying I did!" He then pulled at the door that was already loose at its hinges. It hung to one side and he made no effort to make it even with the door frame.

"You're going to have to fix my door," Liz called after him as he disappeared into the darkness toward Grandpa Bordeaux' cabin. He was more tired now and wished he hadn't gone to Liz's house. He was also uneasy about the axing of White Hat and the police. He decided after a few hour's sleep he would ask around to find out just what had happened to White Hat. He never knew Liz to understand anything as it really happened. He thought: It's probably the same this time, too.

9

Several miles outside of Cut Meat, Shot turned left onto a narrow dirt road that cut across the prairie and joined with the oil-surfaced state highway, Route 20, that connects the eastern part of the state with Rapid City and the Black Hills.

It took only 30 seconds to drive the half-mile to the state highway. At the highway he turned right and headed west toward Rapid City. There was no traffic on the road—it was past 2:30 in the morning. He picked up speed rapidly—70, 80 mph, the miles passed quickly.

Clorine, sitting next to Shot was awake and crying as the pain in her face got worse. The shock had worn off some since leaving Cody. But she said nothing, neither asking to be taken home nor getting out somewhere to find her way back to Cut Meat. Shot hardly noticed she was in the car. He didn't speak to her. He just kept driving faster and more recklessly. Every so often he turned his head to talk with someone in the back seat. The car sped down the highway ricocheting from one side to the other like a bullet gone astray. Somehow it stayed on the road. Vetal, where they were going, was located a few hundred feet beyond the reservation boundary across the county line. Vetal, South Dakota, had a population of about fifteen, all white people who earned their living by ranching some and operating several little businesses: a filling station, general store, and two cafe-bars facing each other across the highway. There was nothing particularly memorable about Vetal. It was like a lot of little towns in South Dakota and Nebraska. There were several small houses and sheds, a couple of trailer houses, an assortment of farm implements in the fields — hay cutters, rakes and the like — and a few aluminum storage bins for grain. But not much more.

When Irish's Bar was in Vetal the place was a great Sunday haunt, with frequent drinking bouts and fights. But when Irish's moved to Mission the town quieted down, and for a few years it attracted mostly white and Indian teenagers, who could easily purchase alcoholic beverages there. But lately more reservation Indians were frequenting the town's two cafe bars, and Vetal once again was developing a reputation to rival those of Crockston, Gordon, Cody, White Clay and others in and around reservations in South Dakota. Most of the Indians at Vetal were from Redridge Reservation, but a few Pine Ridge Sioux (Oglalas) came in from Martin or White Clay. And not so many years ago there were several drunken brawls at Vetal between the Redridge Sioux and the Oglalas from Pine Ridge. The rivalry between the two tribes went back many years. There had even been incidents, before World War II, when the Indian youths from Pine Ridge came in gangs to Redridge to fight and destroy property, and vice versa. While the general dislike between the tribes persisted even to the present, the feelings were not nearly so strong.

Whipple ordered Shot to turn around and go back to the He Dog Dam cutoff they passed several miles back. Shot stopped and tried backing up several times in the center of the narrow road before he could get the car turned around. He spun off in the direction they had just come, still swerving recklessly down the highway, dangerously close to striking the ditches along the edge of the road. He passed the turnoff before he saw it and again had to back up and turn around in the road. Finally he turned off the highway onto a sandy trail that wound its way over the darkened prairie toward the He Dog Dam.

Shot had to stop along the way to open the several barbed wire cattle gates so the car could pass between pastures. It was a relatively simple matter to detach the gate post from the post on which it was fastened, then lay the wire aside and drive the cattle (or car) through, then refasten the gate as it was before. Sometimes, however, resetting the gate was a little problem because it involved pulling up the gate post tight with the fence post, then holding the two together with one hand while trying to fasten them together with a piece of rope or wire hung from one of the posts.

While Shot had set up gates hundreds of times before and knew how angry the ranchers got when they found the gates open, allowing the cattle to move into other pastures, he nevertheless left down the first two gates he came to. But when he got to the third gate he was asleep until the scraping noise of wire against metal and Whipple's calling him "a blind fucking idiot" woke him up. But he had already torn out the gate and had to untangle the wire from the grill and fender. He found the wire had not broken but had simply come loose from the posts.

Some goddamn rancher's going to be madder than a bastard when he sees this mess, he thought. As he went on, the car lights shone onto a little valley as the road dipped. The car turned before it began to climb toward the bluffs surrounding the He Dog Dam, now only a few hundred feet ahead. It was very dark as he came to the top of the little hill, and the lights of the car shone out over the water. He could see the far bank and the bluffs along the shore there.

Another car was parked off to his right with a radio blaring out loud rock music from the powerful radio station KOMA in Oklahoma City. When the music ended a voice came on. It was fast-talking, and was peddling a greaseless ointment guaranteed to dry up pimples and chase away adolescent blues. Then another rock number began.

Whipple was the first out of the car, and Eagle Man and Shot were close behind. Jimmy Little Crow and the two women, Lilly and Clorine, stayed in the car. Lilly was asleep and Clorine was sick and throwing up on the floor in the front seat. Little Crow was quietly sipping gin in the back.

His eyes not accustomed to the darkness, Whipple had difficulty seeing who was in the other car. He was sure they must have a little beer or whiskey. As he got nearer he could smell the beer and recognized Louis LaPointe from Cut Meat sitting behind the wheel. LaPointe was quite drunk and when he saw Whipple, he gave out with a little wave and a queer, nervous laugh.

Whipple ignored Louis for the moment and stuck his arm through the open window to speak to the persons in the back seat saying, "Gimme a beer.'

There were four teenagers in back, the two Yellow Hawk sisters from Cut Meat and two boys from another reservation town. One of the boys, hesitating a moment before he did, trying to get a look at who it was that would dare demand they give him a beer, when he saw it was Whipple, opened a can of beer.

Whipple withdrew his arm. He took a long drink of the cold beer, then another long gulp before tossing the empty can into the water and reaching his arm through the window for another can. Meanwhile, a somewhat sobered-up Louis asked Whipple in a soft voice, so those in the back seat couldn't hear, "What'd you do back in town?" He used his thumb to point in the general direction of Cut Meat behind him.

"Whadda you mean?" Whipple asked, taking another long gulp of beer, finishing the second can and throwing it in the direction of the water, too. It landed in the soft earth along the shore of the reservoir.

"Somebody beat up on White Hat with an ax tonight. He's in the Redridge hospital and in pretty bad shape. He's not gonna make it, I hear. The police are looking for who done it and want to know who was down by his place tonight." Then he let out with that peculiar little laugh of his. Whipple ignored it. "I know you was down there." Louis went on. "But I didn't say nothing about it to them. I figure they can find out for themselves. Did you do it, Ben? Ax White Hat, I mean?." Without waiting for an answer, he kept on. "I know you did it, no one else in town would dare do something that bad except maybe Charlie Crazy Cat and he ain't nowhere around these parts no more.

"Maybe Charlie came back again," Whipple answered, finally, "but you best keep quiet about me doing any axing." His tone of voice, though quiet and unworried, was nevertheless menacing, so that even slow-witted Louis understood what he meant.

"Who you got in the back seat?" Whipple wanted to know, changing the subject, not very concerned about what Louis had been asking. He looked over the two young Yellow Hawk girls.

The girls saw what was on his mind. In Indian, one of them asked Louis to start up the car and leave, hoping Whipple didn't understand much Indian, which he didn't.

But by now Louis was passed out and didn't answer her. Not that he would have left while Whipple wanted him to stay.

Whipple could see a case of beer on the floor and had his mind on the beer as much as the two girls. Finally he opened the car door and started to climb in back. The girls promptly went out the other side of the car and ran off down the road in the dark toward Cut Meat, leaving the two high school boys alone with Whipple. But not for long.

"Get the fuck out of here!" Whipple screamed. "Go find your girl friends."

He laughed as they ran, leaving him with the case of beer. It was unusual for two strong young men to leave a case of beer without a fight. They'd heard of Whipple, and heard Louis talking about the axing of White Hat. And they knew not to fight with him. Whipple got out of the car lugging the case of beer with him. Shot and Eagle Man had returned to the other car and were waiting for Whipple to come back. Louis was asleep behind the wheel.

But instead of going back to the car, Whipple walked over to the edge of the reservoir and sat down on the ground where he could look out over the water and drink the beer all by himself. In the darkness he couldn't see the water, but it was there, he thought. He didn't need to see it to know it was there.

It was near freezing and a cold northeast wind had picked up, making the early morning hours even colder. But he didn't seem bothered by the cold as he drank beer after beer, throwing each can over the edge of the bluff where they would land in the water or on the rocky shore below.

He thought about the White Hat axing with no great regret. He was an old man, he muttered to himself. But it would be unfortunate if the police somehow linked him to it. He didn't see how they could. White Hat couldn't have seen him do it, even though Leo was sure to say it was him, if he lived. But he could deny it and the police would have a hard time proving anything, unless they could find someone who saw him near White Hat's place. Likely no one in the car would dare say anything like that. And if they did he'd make them think again before they testified against him. Finally, he decided things would be a lot less complicated all around if old White Hat died.

He finished the last of the beers and walked back toward the car. He found Shot awake, all over Clorine. Eagle Man and Lilly were huddled together asleep in the back seat and Little Crow was on the floor sleeping, his empty bottle next to him.

Whipple had a good buzz on from the case of beer he had drunk. He didn't want the feeling to end, nearly dawn, he decided it was time they went on to Vetal to be there in time for the opening of the cafe.

"Let's get going," he said to Shot, huddled in the corner with Clorine. "Vetal will be opening soon," he said. "Let's get going."

10

Tuffy was not quite awake when he heard the knock at the door. Through his half-sleep he listened as his grandfather got up to see who was there.

"What do you want with Tuffy?"

The hint of reproach and concern in the voice reminded him that his grandfather cared even though no one else gave a damn whether he lived or died. It was a simple admission of truth he had and would live with, without bitterness.

As his grandfather talked, Tuffy got dressed, preparing to go into the kitchen to answer whatever they had to ask.

There were eight persons sleeping in the room with Tuffy, some two to a bed, and others curled up in blankets on the dirt floor. No one else in the room had been bothered by the noise from the other room. Light began to come through the window across the room. It was cold and muted as if snow were on its way. Tuffy realized that it was almost seven o'clock, and he had been sleeping for nearly four hours. It seemed like five minutes.

He pushed aside the cloth curtain that divided the back room from the kitchen and stepped into the light. Standing in the kitchen were two tribal police officers, his grandfather, and Father Keel. He was surprised to see Father Keel, since he hadn't heard his voice. He entered the little room barefoot, buttoning his

pants. His long black hair hung tangled and down in front of his
eyes. The priest spoke right away.

"We know you didn't do this awful thing, Tuffy, but the police
have the idea you are somehow involved. Your grandfather and I,
we know better of course. We know you aren't that kind of boy, not
the kind to ax an old man like Leo White Hat. I'm going along to
Redridge later to see that you get some help, a good attorney if
you need one."

Tuffy was very confused. It had all come so fast.

"What do you mean?"

"The police believe you had something to do with the axing of
White Hat last night," Grandpa Bordeaux said to him in Indian,
speaking softly and trying not to show alarm at what was
happening. His voice sounded tired, as if the many years
repeated over and over had at long last worn him down. The
weariness of voice and sadness in his eyes made him appear to be
an old man who would welcome dying. An overwhelming fear
caught hold of Tuffy when he suddenly realized he was being
accused of axing Leo White Hat.

"I didn't do nothing to old man White Hat," he stammered to his
grandfather, his voice choking as if about to cry.

"I know you didn't do anything of the kind, Tuffy," his
grandfather answered him, still speaking in Indian and trying to
smile as he spoke. "But the police think you know something and
they want you to go to Redridge with them. I told them you
couldn't have done it, and so did Father Keel. You do what Father
Keel tells you and everything will be all right again."

One of the officers at the door was watching Tuffy closely,
expecting he might try to run away at any moment. He was a big
husky full-blooded Sioux of about thirty-five years. In his hands
he held a black cossack-type hat with ear flaps. He shifted the hat
from hand to hand while he translated the Indian being spoken
for the other officer, Inspector Rifle, who was in charge.

Rifle nodded his head as he heard what was said between Tuffy
and his grandfather. He didn't interrupt, just stood there

watching, taking long draws on his cigarette. But when Tuffy and his grandfather finished talking Rifle spoke to Tuffy in English.

"We ain't saying you did it, son." He spoke with an accent that sounded as though it came out of Wyoming or Utah. "Well, it's just you was seen down by White Hat's last night and we want to talk to you a little more—that's all. I think it's lots easier talking down at my office at Redridge."

He flashed a toothy smile showing his inexpensive dentures that had been purchased at a time when false teeth were made to look unrealistically perfect, like an even white picket fence. "Let's go," he said, ending the conversation and half running out the door toward the car which still had its motor going.

The other officer waited to see what Tuffy would try, expecting trouble at that momemt if it were to come at all. Once Tuffy was in the police car there would be no chance of escape. For a moment Tuffy thought of running, but seeing the officer blocking the doorway and wearing a look that said, try it if you think you can get away with it, he decided to go along without a struggle. As he got in the back of the police car he saw Father Keel walking back toward his house across the gravel road. He hoped the priest wouldn't forget the promise to help him.

11

Tuffy got easily confused when he had to answer any questions and didn't like talking in English, especially with people he didn't know. He felt like they were making fun of the way he spoke. He preferred to speak in Indian—he could make himself understood better.

At the station, after being questioned by the police for several hours, Tuffy had explained over and over again to the police that after getting into the car at Shot's place he couldn't remember anything more until he woke up on his way to Crockston.

The police said they had questioned Louis LaPointe and that he had told them he saw Tuffy at the scene of the crime at about the time it happened. Louis had been questioned, but he simply told the police that he didn't know anything, except that Tuffy was in the car. They said Louis also told them, which, in fact, Louis did not, that Tuffy was passed out drunk in the car, but a few minutes later he'd come around and demanded to be let out in front of White Hat's cabin. He was very angry and crazed looking, so the police told it, and had gotten out of the car while the others drove on to find some women friends. What he'd done there, Louis didn't know, but when Tuffy came back to the car he was quiet, drank some more gin, and passed out again. The police had made up the whole scenario.

"Who are we supposed to believe?" Inspector Rifle asked Tuffy. The police were very thorough in their presentation to Tuffy. Impressing him by the way they told it, they seemed confident it had happened just the way they were telling it to him. And Tuffy had to admit he'd done many crazy things when he was drunk — things he couldn't remember later. Like the time he beat up one of the summer recreation workers who came to the reservation from Augustana College in Sioux Falls. He didn't remember a minute of that incident, but there was no doubt he'd done it.

But to near kill a man with an ax, especially a man he had no quarrel with, well, that wasn't possible, unless he was really provoked. And he hadn't been, as far as he could remember. But if it weren't true, why in hell would Louis say such a thing? There wasn't any trouble between them. It just didn't make sense.

It was all very confusing to him as the questioning went on. And the priest — the prick, he thought — never showed up, nor did that real fine lawyer he promised ever come.

12

The horizon to the east was becoming a fiery red and the sky all
around had the gray, deathlike hue that came in February and
March. Shot drove along the narrow road. He passed the barbed
wire gate he had knocked down going in. When the car reached
the state highway, Route 20, he turned right and again headed in
the direction of Vetal, where the cafe-bars would be opening in
less than half an hour. It was now a few minutes after seven and
getting light.

The reservation region is located in the Mountain Standard
Time Zone, near the Central Standard Time Zone. The exact point
of change comes at Carter, South Dakota, a point midway
between Winner and Mission on the east side of the reservation.
Everyone on the reservation should be on Mountain Time instead
of Central Time, but everyone uses fast time, so that sunrise and
sunset in the winter are later. Sunset doesn't come until after six
o'clock in the wintertime.

Shot was still zig-zagging down the road. He met several cars
coming in the opposite direction, but they wisely pulled off to the
shoulder until he passed by.

It was a very cold morning. There was no wind and the cold
seemed to penetrate everything alive. Ahead, spread out in every
direction as far as the eye could see, was the brown tundra-like
plain, sometimes flat, sometimes slightly hilly. Hundreds of

miles of this drab, brown land wouldn't come alive for another six weeks or more. Most of it was not inhabited or even used, except for an occasional ranch house far out on the prairie or a remote Indian village here and there.

Ordinarily it took only about ten minutes to drive from the He Dog Dam cutoff to Vetal, but Shot made it in something less than six minutes. Except for Eagle Man and Whipple, and Shot who was driving, everyone else was asleep in the car. Clorine lay across the front seat, her legs pulled up under her and her head pushing against Shot's hip. She slept soundly, no longer sobbing. Her nose was broken and flattened, one eye closed tight, and dried, caked blood surrounded her nose and mouth. She was certain to have some very ugly scars, without medical attention. Likely she would let the cuts heal without help of any kind.

Jimmy Little Crow, the hunchback, was still on the floor in the back seat. He was passed out with an empty bottle next to his lips.

Bleary-eyed drunk and almost asleep behind the wheel, Shot drove into Vetal, not slowing very much as he passed the gas station on the edge of town just before the cafe-bar.

"Where the fuck you going, you asshole?" Whipple screamed. Shot slammed on the brakes and turned slightly to the right until he was on the cinders and then slid sideways for about twenty-five yards before stopping in front of the cafe. The arrival woke everyone in the car and Whipple continued to curse him, accusing him of trying to kill them all with his crazy driving.

Their arrival brought the wife of the cafe owner to the window to see what all the noise was about. She wasn't surprised to see a carload of Indians sitting in the parking lot. Seldom a morning went by when there wasn't a car full of Indians out front coming from nearby Redridge or sometimes from Pine Ridge Reservation. Some mornings she remembered seeing that parking lot damn near full of Indian cars waiting for the cafe to open.

She turned away disgusted at what she saw, knowing that in a few minutes she would have to wait on them. It was a sin she thought.

For the first time all night Whipple slept. While they waited for the cafe to open its doors no one spoke in the car. Noone noticed another car's arrival. In it were three Sioux from Pine Ridge Reservation, all drunk. Like Whipple, Shot and the rest, they were waiting to buy more liquor at Vetal.

The cafe opened promptly at 7:30, and as the door opened, Whipple was miraculously awake and out of the car. He stretched his arms and yawned. Then he noticed the other car, strangers all of them.

Shot and Eagle Man were out of the car, too, and the three walked toward the cafe door. Shot pulled out three single dollar bills from his pocket. He was the only one with any money left.

The Indians in the other car met them at the entrance to the cafe. The three were much drunker than Shot, Whipple, or Eagle Man. They also seemed to be in ugly moods. Reaching for the door at the same time, the half dozen Indians scuffled to see who would be the first inside, with Whipple holding back the three Pine Ridge Indians until Shot and Eagle Man and himself were inside. Once inside the cafe the Pine Ridge trio insisted on being first at the counter, and Whipple didn't permit it. Finally, a little angry, Whipple picked up the smallest of the three and threw him against a juke box in the corner, cracking the glass over the tune selector. Before more trouble could develop, however, the owner of the cafe had come in from the back room.

"You sons of bitches ain't going to break up my place," he hollered. "Get out of here before I call the highway patrol!"

"We didn't mean you any trouble, Mr. Desmet," Eagle Man said, hoping to calm him down so they could buy the beer. He hoped that old man Desmet might remember him, because he had done some painting for Desmet which at the time seemed to please him. It was awhile ago but he thought he might still remember.

And Whipple said, "Yeah, all we want is a little beer and we'll be going along." Shot didn't say anything, nor did the three Pine Ridge Indians. The man Whipple had thrown against the juke box was on his feet and unhurt, and Desmet didn't notice the cracked glass on the juke box.

"Give them what they want," he said to his wife, who had come out from the back to help if she could. "But this place is closing to your kind — we don't want any more of your business. Go back to the reservation."

While his wife was in the back getting the beer out of the cooler a bus pulled up in front of the gas pumps. It looked to Desmet like a cross-country express bus. Buses seldom stopped for fuel, although quite a number of big trucks had been coming in lately since he now had diesel fuel. When a bus stopped it usually meant mechanical trouble of some kind. So after giving the Indians their beer he went out to the gas pumps to help the driver. The repair was simple, a loose belt, and the driver seemed to know just what to do. In the meantime, the passengers, welcoming the opportunity to get off the bus, had gone into the cafe for something to eat. There were about eighteen passengers, and for about a half hour the cafe owner and his wife prepared coffee and eggs for the hungry group, most of whom had been riding all night. Some of them noticed the colorful Sioux beadwork on the shelf behind the lunch counter — rosettes, necklaces, beaded wallets, and earrings.

"Are they genuine Indian-made?" someone wanted to know.

"Sure are," the cafe owner answered, friendly and smiling for the first time that morning, as he saw an opportunity to get rid of some of the junk he had accumulated over the past few months. Maybe at a good return, too, he thought. Usually the items were pawned by the reservation Indians for gas for their cars, or more likely, a six pack of beer. The dealing always was very one-sided, with Desmet trading seventy-five cents or a dollar's worth of something for a beaded rosette worth at least three dollars in a souvenir store. But he had to wait to get his price.

"Genuine Indian-made by our Sioux people on the reservation," he said, going into his sales pitch. "Talented people they are, able to produce items that can't be duplicated anywhere else in the world, and cheap, too." He pulled down the necklaces, rosettes, and other items, taking special care not to show the rosette with 'Made in Hong Kong' stamped on the back. He bought that one from a Sioux, only to discover later its true origin printed for all to see. He was still looking for the squaw who sold him that piece of beadwork. He gave a dollar and a quarter for it. Not that it wasn't good work; the craftmanship was every bit as good as something Sioux-made, probably even better than much of that made by the younger Indian women. The simple truth was that the work done by the majority of the Indian beaders was inferior to that coming out of the Orient. While the work of an old Sioux beader couldn't be improved on, the stuff sold at the border towns was not very good. Often it was made hastily for a little liquor. There was little pride of good craftsmanship left.

Desmet sold a lot of the craft work he had accumulated on his shelf. He wished he had more to sell. As the passengers left the cafe for the bus, they passed by the two cars with the Indians inside. Some people peered inside the car windows, a little curious as to who would be sitting drinking beer in front of a cafe at eight o'clock on a Sunday morning, but no one said anything.

Nevertheless, before all the passengers were on the bus, one of the Pine Ridge Indians got out of his car, picked up a stone, threw it and barely missed hitting the head of a middle-aged cowboy; the stone hit the side of the bus with a loud thud.

In a moment other Indians were throwing stones, beer cans and anything else they could lay their hands on.

As the startled tourists scrambled to get on the bus, several persons were hit, but no one was seriously injured. Finally, everyone was safely aboard and the driver closed the door quickly and drove away. Eight Indians stood on the edge of the road, cold sober in their open hatred, hurling objects at the side of the bus as it moved away in the direction of Rapid City and the Black Hills.

Seeing Desmet on the porch with his shotgun leveled at them, the Indians scurried back to their cars. Shot headed east in the direction of Redridge. The Pine Ridge Indians drove west, coming up behind the bus and passing it by at about eighty mph.

13

The sun was higher now and had warmed the prairie. The dead grasses were brown-buff, with just a streak of green appearing here and there. It was suddenly more habitable than the hours before dawn, when there was only the bone-chilling windless cold spreading over the barren uninviting land.

Most of the way back, the road was straight except for a gentle sweep to the right four or five miles outside Vetal. Shot was following the yellow line in the center of the road, a wheel on each side. He hadn't slowed any, but now seemed able to follow a reasonably straight path.

Whipple had already drunk one of the six packs of beer, with Eagle Man getting one or two cans. They were now into the second six pack, and Eagle Man handed a can to Shot as they got nearer to the old Cut Meat road.

As he approached the turnoff Shot slowed almost to a stop, remembering the dip at the beginning of the road and the ruts left from a pickup truck that got stuck in the mud during the January thaw. The cold spell that came a week after the thaw froze those wheel ruts solid. It was a narrow road, part sand and clay, a solid foundation, except during a hard rain or a quick winter thaw. The road was straight except for the first two hundred feet, where a little hill blocked the view ahead.

The car nearly stalled as they started up the incline. Then as Shot pushed the accelerator to the floor it hesitated and moved ahead, straining. It slowly gained speed as they came closer to the crest of the hill. The exhaust was loud and the rods in the engine were clanking, sounding as though they might come out through the side at any moment.

Over the top of the hill the road was straight and level, until it reached the old Cut Meat road two miles east of the village. As they came over the crest of the hill they met head-on with a blue Chevrolet pickup truck traveling at about sixty miles an hour.

The front end of Shot's Chevy was lifted several feet off the ground and pushed back down the hill; the car rolled end over end several times until it came to a stop at the bottom near the ruts in the frozen ground, not far from Route 20. Shot and Clorine in the front seat were killed instantly. Jimmy Little Crow, the hunchback, was thrown through a window and suffered minor injuries. Lilly Crow Dog lay next to the wrecked auto, choking on her own blood. She died several minutes later.

Whipple and Eagle Man, sitting low in the back seat sipping beer when they hit, were thrown against the seat ahead. Eagle Man was dead immediately. Whipple, near death, was rushed to the Redridge Hospital where he was transferred to St. Elizabeth's Hospital in Rapid City.

In the pickup truck there were six people, and all six died. Two men and a woman were sitting in the cab. The driver was Tuffy's Uncle Ralph, who was on his way to Vetal for more beer after a night of partying in Cut Meat. With him were the Broken Lances, also from Cut Meat, and huddled together in one blanket on the back platform of the pickup were the Broken Lances' three children. The oldest was nine.

After the collision the pickup had rolled on its side and then onto its back, crushing the children.

Whipple and Jimmy Little Crow were the only ones left alive 15 minutes after the impact.

It was not the worst tragedy in South Dakota that weekend. On another Sioux reservation, fifteen Indians died in a fiery crash. As at Redridge, almost everyone involved had been drinking, except for the children.

14

The next night ten bodies were laid out in the Cut Meat American Legion Hall. In the Sioux custom, relatives came from all over. Aunts and uncles, nieces, nephews and cousins came from Denver, Chicago, Cleveland, and other far-away cities.

Wreaths of artificial flowers were placed around the caskets. On a table in the center of the hall was a crucifix with candles around it. Handmade star quilts hung on the wall behind several of the caskets, and there were flags draped over the two coffins of the veterans, Harry Shot and Ralph Bordeaux. Rifles were stacked in a pile next to the flag-draped coffins.

Pictures of the deceased in happier days were put on top of the coffins, but no coffins were opened because the bodies had been broken and torn.

About 9:30 Father Keel and an Episcopal priest by the name of Father Burger arrived and led a prayer ceremony. Seven of the deceased were Roman Catholic, and three Episcopalians. Following the prayer service there was a rosary, Scripture readings, and Lakota hymns.

Usually before leaving a funeral the priests said a few words of consolation to the family and friends of the deceased. The messages usually were brief. But Father Keel was angry and disgusted by the senseless dying that plagued the town.

So after Father Burger delivered his short message, Father Keel stood up and spoke, deciding it was fit and proper that he give the town hell for what was happening. Most of the members of the community were there at that hour.

"As we gather here to grieve over our losses in this tragic and senseless auto wreck my thoughts turn to another tragedy that was visited upon us this weekend. I refer to the axing of Leo White Hat who now lies in the Redridge Hospital and is not expected to live.

"You all know of course the police have apprehended a suspect—young Tuffy Bordeaux. Many of us think it unlikely Tuffy did it, and we can't presume guilt until he is tried by a panel of his peers—a jury—in the best tradition of what America stands for. But probably it won't get that far, and I hope it won't."

"Nevertheless, let us for a moment presume the worst, that is, that Tuffy did do it, that awful cowardly deed. Was not his mind muddled and confused by the effects of alcohol, just as were the minds of those who lie here tonight? Of course I don't mean the children. They are the innocent ones.

"But are not the acts of violence, such as Tuffy is accused of, to be expected when the example set by the adults of this community is one of violence, dishonesty, and never-ending alcoholism? What was done to White Hat was senseless.

"I am reminded of a passage. Many of you know it—'Woe to the man responsible for this deed. It were better he had never been born, or a millstone hung around his neck and he were drowned in the depths of the sea.'"

No one moved after the priest finished. Tuffy's grandfather sat in the corner listening and watching, puffing a cigarette quietly and not talking to anyone.

After a while an Indian rose and led the gathering in singing Lakota hymns, and various friends and relatives got up between hymns and gave testimony to the goodness of the deceased. At midnight, the singing and eulogizing ended and food was put out—coffee, meat, cakes, sandwiches, fried bread, and wosapi, an indian pudding. Nearly everyone went home after having something to eat except for close relatives and those from out of town who had no place to go. They would stay the night through.

15

Tuffy was questioned all day. Police Inspector Rifle did most of the talking, and changed his approach several times. He began by being stern and serious, reminding Tuffy that another Indian boy was soon to be executed for killing a shopkeeper (a white man) in Sioux Falls. When that didn't bring a confession, he softened up and talked to Tuffy as an understanding parent or teacher and tried to convince the confused boy that as a police officer he was only concerned for his welfare. He explained that the courts would be very lenient with someone who was cooperative, meaning that if he would confess to axing White Hat he would have an easier time of it.

Under Rifle's questioning Tuffy was weakening. Tuffy didn't see how he could have done such an awful thing, but he had to admit at least to himself that there was a possibility he had done it. He could do some pretty cruel things when he was drunk.

The good lawyer Father Keel promised never came. Father Keel had been serious about his promise, but after talking with his good friend Inspector Rifle, a man whom he considered honest and fair in his dealings with the Indian people, he agreed that if a lawyer were brought in right away the cause of justice might not be served, and explained how some lawyers had a way of impeding justice with all their legal maneuvering.

While what the police inspector said didn't exactly fit Father Keel's concept of justice, he thought that a lot of criminals were being set free on legal technicalities, which was as contrary to the American system as was denying a man an attorney. He was undecided until the inspector said Tuffy would likely get sent to a training school (because he was only seventeen), and be sent away from the alcohol and other problems that got him into so much trouble on the reservation. The priest saw sense in that and decided justice might better be served if he delayed a few days in getting Tuffy the lawyer he had promised. There was a lot of time yet before even a hearing could be held at the Rapid City Federal Court.

Without a lawyer, Tuffy saw no hope and agreed to confess. That day Inspector Rifle called in a FBI agent to witness the taking of a confession from Tuffy. Tuffy was to admit to axing Leo White Hat. The agent was there to see that everything was done legally. Tuffy swore before the agent that it was he who had axed Leo White, thinking things could get no worse.

That night, White Hat died.

Apple-wood Press began in January 1976.
The image of the apple joined with the hard concreteness of wood in many ways expresses the goals of the press. One of the first woods used in printing, apple-wood remains a metaphor for giving ideas a form. Apple-wood Press books are published in the memory of Harry and Lillian Apple.